TODAY'S A YELLOW DAY

TODAY'S A YELLOW DAY

JAMES ROTH

ILibrary of Congress Control Number:		2012908817
ISBN:	Hardcover	978-1-4771-1351-6
	Softcover	978-1-4771-1350-9
	Ebook	978-1-4771-1352-3

To order additional copies of this book, contact:
Xlibris Corporation
1-888-795-4274
www.Xlibris.com
Orders@Xlibris.com
112463

First, I want to thank my wife for her belief in me and her unwavering support in this new endeavor.

A special thanks goes to Ed Kozemchak for convincing me to continue the effort after reading my first thirty pages.

I must thank Diane Galuppo, our Chief Editor, for her direction, advice, enthusiasm, and endless support in editing the manuscript.

For support in understanding the workings of the police department, I would like to thank the Dobbs Ferry Police force. I am grateful to Lieutenant James Guarnieri and Sergeant Manual Guevera for sharing their knowledge of 1960 police procedures and crime scene investigation with me.

Many family members and friends read the manuscript at various stages. I want to thank you all for your help and support. I am especially grateful to the following people who made significant suggestions or helped edit the many versions of my draft: Diane Galuppo, Casey Cobb, Michelle Roth, Ed Kozemchak, Gerry Guiro, and Mike Cobb. Thank you all.

The values by which we are to survive are not rules for just and unjust conduct, but are those deeper illuminations in whose light justice and injustice, good and evil, means and ends are seen in fearful sharpness of outline.

—Jacob Bronowski

Chapter 1

Today's a Yellow Day

Tim slowly opens his eyes. It is Wednesday morning and the beginning of a beautiful fall day. He lies still for a moment, looking out his bedroom window. He is eighteen and has been lifting weights and working out for five years. The effort has finally proven fruitful. He has grown seven inches in the last two years and gained forty-five pounds. His 150 lb body is electrically charged and ready to go the instant he wakes. He begins to think about the day's scheduled events before his eyes are open.

Today's a yellow day, he decides after getting a full breath of the fresh fall air entering from the slightly opened bedroom window. He jumps out of bed and slips on a yellow shirt, blue jeans, and yellow socks. He flips on the radio, runs into the bathroom, brushes his teeth, combs his hair, washes his face and hands, and returns to his room in three and a half minutes. He grabs his books and quietly walks down the narrow hall. As he passes his parents' room, he notices the door is open. His mother must be up. He descends the stairs hoping to hear her singing. When he reaches the bottom of the stairs, he can see her figure in the den on the couch, and she is quiet.

Walking slowly into the den, he comes up behind her and touches her shoulder. Her head is lowered, and when she turns, she is crying. "Mom, are you okay?" he softly asks, knowing full well she isn't.

"I don't know when this will end. Why am I so depressed, again? I hate when you see me like this. I'm so useless," she manages to say through a sea of sighs in a weak voice that sounds like it is ready to break.

"Did you take your pills, Mom?"

"Yes, but they aren't working."

"Maybe, if you get up and move around, you'll feel better."

"No. I can't move. I don't have any energy. What is the use of living? I should be dead."

"Mom, you always talk like this when you're down. Don't say these things! You'll come out of this in a short time." He sits down next to her, and she leans her head on his shoulder.

"Hey, look what color today is!" he exclaims as he points to his shirtsleeve.

"It's a yellow day today for me, and it should be a yellow day for you!"

She moves slightly away from him to get a better look at him, and a small smile breaks through her aging Irish face. Five years back, before her attacks of depression began, she was often mistaken for her thirty-year-old niece. Now she looks more like her age of fifty-one.

"Yellow is for the sunshine. This is going to be a shiny bright yellow day. How can we miss, and I can see that Irish smile you're trying to hide," Tim adds.

Almost immediately, her sobbing stops. He puts his arm around her shoulder, and they sit motionless for a few quiet minutes.

"I have to go now, or I'll be late. You're going to have to give it your best shot to get out of this today. I know you can do it. I'll be shining yellow all day, and so will you!" He looks back to make sure his dog, Daisy, is safely in the house before he closes the front door behind him.

Tim leaps off the front porch, sprints through the front yard, and turns left down the center of the street, Mohican Park Avenue. Over the past five years, he learned to leave what happens in the home at home when he closes the door behind him. He is halfway through the football season, and the effects of the training have put a quick stride in his step.

It is midway through October and the leaves have begun to change. Mohican Park Avenue has maple trees on both sides of the street. The trees are old, have grown to full size, and create a tunnel of yellow, orange, and red colors that partially block the sun. The houses along the street reflect the largely blue-collar and middle-class neighborhood, while the fifty-year-old maple trees, which line the street, create a dramatic tunnel of fall foliage that Tim enjoys walking through each morning on the way to school.

Dobbs Ferry is a picturesque village that borders the Hudson River and is only about twenty miles north of New York City. It was named after Jeremiah Dobbs, who, prior to and during the American Revolutionary War, would ferry travelers across the

Hudson River. It is one of six villages that mostly border the Hudson River and form the Town of Greenburgh in the county of Westchester, New York. The Town of Greenburgh was established in 1788. Prior to 1788, it was a part of Philipsburg Manor. Since the owners of Philipsburg Manor were Tories during the revolution, their properties were confiscated after the war, and the name Philipsburg was changed to Greenburgh.

In the eighteen hundreds, city dwellers would take day trips on sailboats north and visit the river town's villages, including Hastings on the Hudson, Dobbs Ferry, Irvington, and Tarrytown, as a means of weekend relaxation. This period of Dobbs Ferry's history, as a weekend resort destination, might explain why there are so many restaurants and bars in the village.

It has a quaint business district with a main street that has a beautiful view of the Palisades. The Palisades are famous cliffs that line the west side of the Hudson River. Main Street starts a block from the Hudson River and runs uphill north to Cedar Street. Cedar Street runs a short distance east to Ashford Avenue, and Ashford Avenue continues east for a mile and a half to the inland neighboring village of Ardsley. Blue-collar and middle-income families own the homes along Main Street, Cedar Street, Ashford Avenue, and the adjoining streets. A majority of the rest of the village includes the upper-middle and wealthy-income families with executives that commute to New York City.

The Old Croton Aqueduct runs from Croton on the Hudson south through Dobbs Ferry and continues to New York City. It once acted as the main supply of water to New York City. The aqueduct remains as a hiking trail and has an access point at the top end of Main Street at the intersection of Main and Cedar Streets. The students that live in the Main Street area of the village use the aqueduct as a shortcut route to the high school. The back parking lot of the school faces the aqueduct and has stairs leading to the aqueduct.

The entire village is only two square miles. His home is less than a half-mile from the high school. The Ferrari house has always been open to any of Veronica and Bob Ferrari's friends or their children's friends at any time of the day or night, and they have been coming for years. Since Veronica always offers tea to show her hospitality, the Ferrari home became known as Ferrari's teahouse when Tim was thirteen.

At eighteen years, Tim has barely ventured outside the confines of the village. He has only once been on a vacation with his mother, and other than an evening at a lake, he has never been on vacation with his father. The village is twenty miles north of Grand Central Station in New York City, yet he has been to New York City only three times in his life. Despite his lack of exposure to the world, he is, in many ways, not wanting for anything.

Dobbs Ferry offers parks and activities during the summer. There are a number of ponds for fishing. The Hudson provides saltwater fishing, crabbing, and boating. Five years back, at age thirteen, Tim and a number of friends became caddies at the local country club, giving them access to the golf course on Caddies Day every Monday during the summer. In his three years of high school, aside from making money caddying, he has shoveled snow during the winter, sold homemade candelabras for Christmas, washed and polished cars, mowed lawns during the summer, helped clean the movie theater, had a paper route, and worked as a soda jerk at Kessler's drug store. The village offers many ways to earn extra cash, and Tim has seldom been without money during his high school years.

Despite being unusually small for football in his first three years of high school, Tim managed to stay on the team and play some junior varsity football. Having grown in his junior year, he is starting on varsity offense and defense in his senior year.

Dobbs Ferry is a village that more than loves its sports. It is suffering from sports mania. The people of the village support the players by filling the stands, as well as making positive and negative comments before, during, and after the games. High school football is a village obsession and a right of passage for the players. Most of the village football support comes from the blue-collar and middle-income families.

Many of these families have lived in the village for two to five generations, and there are close ties among them. They consider themselves as local villagers. Local villagers are permanent residents that best represent the village's culture. Families that move into the village, when their children are young and leave when their children have grown, are viewed as transients by the local villagers. Their cultural heritage is mostly Italian and Irish and, in recent years, Jewish. The village reflects the cultural makeup with an abundance of pizza parlors, Italian delis, Italian bakeries, Irish pubs, and Jewish-owned hardware, clothing, and drug stores. It is in this setting that Tim has spent his entire life, and on this fall day of 1960, Tim is about to have a yellow day.

Chapter 2

The Fate of a Rat

Tito Menetti suddenly wakes from a deep sleep. It is 8:15a.m. If he doesn't rush to get up and out the door, his father will catch him leaving late for school. What his father doesn't know is that Tito hasn't been to school for months. He was expelled at the beginning of the semester for brutally beating a student. Tito's mother has not informed his father of the situation out of fear of the beating he will give his son.

Despite his need to rush, Tito slowly turns over and looks out his bedroom window. His sharp eyesight immediately notices movement in the backyard. A rat slowly, almost arrogantly, walks between two garbage cans. Lower Main Street has had an infestation of rats since the village closed the local dump just a short distance from lower Main Street. Tito quietly opens the window, grabs his pellet gun, aims at the rat, and slowly squeezes the trigger.

He grins as the pellet slams into the neck of the rat. He quickly climbs out the back window and jumps off the back porch, still in his underwear. The pellet is only strong enough to knock the rat out, and Tito has only a minute or two to act. He grabs garden gloves from the backyard shed, along with a hammer and a few nails. He places the rat against the wall of the shed and hammers one, a second, and finally, a third nail into the rat's legs. He quickly grabs a ladder from the side of his house, climbs back onto the back porch roof, and crawls back through the window into his bedroom. He sits quietly by the window again, only now the grin is gone. It is replaced with turned down lips and a hollow stare as he watches the rat slowly die.

Tito was born to abysmal poverty and an abusive and illiterate father, Mario. His father's excessive drinking frequently leads to brutal beatings of his mother or to him.

Tito is void of any feelings for his mother or father. His father's cruelty has drained him of any normal reactions to affection or caring about other human beings.

Realizing it is getting late, he dresses and attempts to leave the house without being seen, but his father is sitting at the kitchen table, and there is no way to exit without Mario seeing him. Before Tito can get to the front door, Mario grabs him around the neck and throws him against the wall using one arm to keep his head pinned to the wall.

"If I catch you late for school one more time, you will go through the window instead of out the door," he growls with his face three inches from Tito's face. Fearing Tito is about to receive a beating, Tito's mother, Carla, interrupts, "I asked him to clean his room before he leaves. That is why he is late." Mario loosens his grip on Tito, swings around, and delivers a hard backhand to Carla's face. "Shut up and stay out of this," Mario responds, while Tito slips out the front door without looking back.

He walks south down lower Main Street toward the Hudson River. He wants to join up with Marco Devito, who hangs out by the river dump and often has a special gift for Tito. As Tito passes the train station for the Hudson River line carrying commuters to and from New York City, John Romano, one of Dobbs Ferry's finest, spots him. Officer Romano leans back in his squad car. "There goes trouble," he tells his partner Ray McEntire.

The village has created a small park next to the train station and has closed the dump at the north end of the park but has not covered it up yet. The plans are to cover the dump with landfill, but they must get rid of the rat problem first before they complete the project to avoid half the village, including Main Street from being invaded by the remaining rats from the rat-infested dump.

Tito walks north toward the park. As he approaches the dump, he can see Marco waiting for him. Marco has emigrated from Italy only five years ago. He has a thick Italian accent and a thick body to match. He stands five feet seven inches tall, weighs 185 pounds, and is all muscle. Despite his massive frame, he has a dark-skinned baby face below his thick brown hair making him look far more innocent than he is. His walk lends more to his darker side. He is muscle-bound and lacks coordination, so when he walks, he seems to sway from side to side giving him a tougher image.

"I don't have any gift for you today," Marco yells out in broken English as Tito approaches.

"Why not?" Tito asks.

"I didn't have the time to find one. There is a golf tournament today at the Ardsley Country Club. I need to make some money caddying. I have to go there, now. The tournament lasts until Sunday. I'll have something for you on Monday morning."

The gift Tito is expecting is usually a stray dog or cat that Tito will tie to the train tracks and watch the commuter train decapitate it. Tito isn't happy with the absence of a gift, but the morning episode with the arrogant rat has satisfied his need to control the life and death of another living thing for now. Tito joins Marco for a walk through the woods toward the golf course.

The woods run from the Hudson River east to the Old Croton Aqueduct and north to the Ardsley Country Club. It is a large track of land; one of many properties owned by the Rockefellers throughout Westchester County. The woods are dense with trees over a hundred years old, making it difficult sometimes to see someone just a few yards away.

Before the Dutch settled the area in the 1600s, the Weckquaesgeek Indians inhabited it for centuries, and the area was known as Weckquaesguck. The woods are still full of Indian arrowheads, and Indian burial sites that have, long ago, lost their markings. There is something eerily threatening about these woods. They give off indescribable warnings to stay out and create a gloomy ominous feeling once entered. Just four miles north is the woods that inspired Washington Irving to write the book, *The Legend of Sleepy Hollow*. When you step off the aqueduct and enter the woods, it is easy to understand why Washington Irvington wrote about a headless horseman who rides through the woods at night and terrorizes the local inhabitants.

When they reach the Croton Aqueduct, Tito stays behind, while Marco continues north on the aqueduct in the direction of the golf course. Tito, remaining in the woods, stops just short of the back entrance to the high school at a large maple tree where, without being seen, he can easily observe the female students that regularly use the aqueduct to access the school.

Chapter 3

There but for the Grace of God

Tim takes his time walking down his street. The yellow, red, and orange leaves seem to be a little brighter today. When he reaches the end of his block, he can see Johnny Pacetti walking down Ashford Avenue. Johnny waves and waits for Tim to join up with him. Johnny is over six feet tall, has a big frame with long legs, a slightly protruding stomach, and feet that point out. His face is long and his hair is unmanaged, making him look a little like Goofy.

Johnny's eyebrows lift and his eyes open wide, while he sucks in air before he speaks. It always appears as though he needs extra air to talk. "Tim Ferrari, how are you?" he asks in a long drawn-out voice. Johnny has an IQ of about eighty-five, but he never lets it get in the way of his broad smile or his general good feeling about being alive. A wide smile lights up his face. "How is your sister, Jane? Jane was born on May 31, 1941. What is Jane doing these days?" he asks.

Despite Johnny's gift to be able to recall the birthdays of everyone he has ever met, along with an endless amount of other trivia, he will never reach the mental capabilities of an eleven year old. Tim and John are about the same age. Tim has known John for as long as he can remember, and John has always maintained a happy to see you attitude. John has unknowingly taught Tim a simple life lesson. If you think life can be difficult, look around. You are certain to find someone under far more difficult circumstances.

Most of the people in the village treat Johnny with respect, knowing his limitations. However, there are a few individuals, including Tito, who take great joy in belittling him or taking money from him. Once Tim witnessed Marco Devito strip Johnny of seven dollars he had just received after spending half the day caddying. Tim couldn't help thinking, *we will*

all be judged someday on how well we treated the
weakest among us.

Before Tim can respond to Johnny's question about his sister Jane, Johnny notices a bus coming up Ashford Avenue. Again, his dark wide eyebrows lift, his eyes open wide, and he inhales before he speaks.

"Here comes the Yonkers to White Plains 109 bus arriving at Dobbs Ferry at 8:23 a.m., stopping in Ardsley at 8:52 a.m., stopping in Elmsford at 9:17 a.m., and arriving in White Plains at 9:42 a.m."

Not wanting the entire schedule of the Westchester bus lines, Tim asks, "Where are you going today?" "There's a golf tournament today, and I'm going to make a loop," Johnny explains. A loop is a caddy term for carrying a golf bag for one round of golf. Tim tells Johnny he has to go to school and that it is nice to see him. Johnny's eyes open wide. "There is another golf tournament on Sunday. Maybe I'll see you there."

There aren't many chances for Tim to caddy in October. A golf tournament will almost guarantee he will get at least one loop. He can use the extra money, and Sunday is the only day he has free time during the football season.

"Thanks for the lead, Johnny," Tim calls back as he continues on his way to school.

Tim's brief encounters with Johnny often end with the same quiet moment of thought, *There but for the grace of God, go I.*

Chapter 4

In a Brief Horrifying Moment

Tito remains in the woods, only a short distance from the students as they leave the aqueduct to climb the back steps to the high school parking lot. Here, he has a view of the many female students passing on their way to school that never know they are within a few arms length from his grasp. His mind races with thoughts of controlling and dominating each girl that draws his attention. A higher lever of anxiety swells up inside him when each of his chosen girls passes by him. Adding to his frustration, the chosen girls are surrounded by other students.

He is about to leave when Rosanne Carrero, walking alone, slowly comes into his view. It is 9:00 a.m., and she is late for class. There is no one in front of her or behind her. Rosanne has a striking figure. She is lean and well proportioned. While she isn't tall, she is very shapely, and her clothes tend to accent her finely chiseled figure and exceptional good looks. She wears very little makeup on her flawless Italian face. Her beautiful looks do not hide her overall tough attitude, and she doesn't take much grief from anyone. Tito's breathing becomes heavier as she approaches, but he knows he has to maintain control of himself and his constant need for domination.

When Rosanne is about to pass by him, she stops. She loosens her belt, so she can adjust her skirt then reaches under the skirt to adjust her underwear. Her shapely dark legs glisten in the morning sun. Without warning, Tito is on her from behind, pulling her backward into the woods. "Don't look back, or I'll kill you," he growls while pushing her head into the ground and slapping her in the back of the head to reinforce his command. Rosanne doesn't scream or look back.

Tito lifts her legs to a kneeling position and rips off her underwear. He enters her from behind and reaches a climax within seconds. Having satisfied his lust, his insatiable and uncontrollable need to dominate subsides. Rosanne's instincts, not to fight, may have saved her life. Resisting will only excite him. He quickly gets up, pulls up his pants, and disappears into the woods.

In a brief less than three minute horrifying encounter, Rosanne's life will change forever. In a village where no one locks their doors, and the biggest crime on any given day may result in a speeding ticket or a DWI, rape is unimaginable, yet in an instant it has happened to her.

She quickly gets to her feet and runs to the top of the steps that separate the aqueduct and the school parking lot. She reaches the top of the stairs, and then sits down. What has just happened to her begins to have its full impact. Her body is trembling. She strives to collect her thoughts. She decides she can't tell anyone. The shame of what has happened to her is overwhelming. "Who will believe me? Will they think I brought it on myself?" she mumbles to herself. She can't stop shaking. It happened so fast, her skirt is hardly soiled, but her underwear is missing, so she can't go to school. Returning home now is impossible. Her mother is certain to know something is wrong.

Despite her state of mind, she pulls herself up and walks slowly to the front of the high school, turns right on Broadway, and continues walking down to Ashford Avenue and onto Cedar Street, where she enters a clothing store. She manages to control her shaking and is able to purchase underwear. By now, she is in total denial of what has happened and decides to return to school.

When she enters the school, the reality of what has happened to her is beginning to take control again, and she rushes to the girl's locker room. She quickly undresses and heads to the showers. The cold shower cleanses her of the odor of the beast that has attacked her and helps her to calm down and collect her thoughts. She decides to remain in school all day, so she will have recovered enough to face her mother without telling her what happened or breaking down.

No one is going to know what happened to me. No one! You sick demented freak, Tito. You couldn't disguise your voice, and you will pay, she thinks while the cold shower water runs down her motionless bruised and aching body.

Rosanne has found her inner strength, and her denial is quickly changing to thoughts of revenge.

Chapter 5

A New Girl down The Hall

Tim arrives at the high school with two minutes to spare. He gets to his homeroom in time for attendance, and then heads out to his hall monitor assigned location on the third floor. His primary responsibility is to ensure that students proceed to class in an orderly fashion—no running, no fighting, etc. The hall monitor positions are given to seniors more as a means of socializing than to keep order. At 8:45 a.m., the first period bell rings, and the students flood the school corridors on their way to first period classes. They have five minutes to get there.

"Hey, like the colors," Tim hears a recognizable voice say. It is Starkey. Starkey is a nickname that is short for Starkman. Bob Starkman is a little less than six feet tall, has curly black hair, plays outside tackle on the football team, and is known for his hot Jewish temper. Starkey and Tim met the first week Starkey moved to Dobbs Ferry from New York City when they were thirteen. Their chance meeting was at a bicycle pump. Starkey grabbed the pump hose before Tim had finished using it. When Tim protested, Starkey hit him over the head with a cast he had on his left arm. A vicious fight ensued that ended in a draw. It would be the first of endless fights they would have over the next five years. In those five years they have become close friends, separated only by their constant need to compete. Starkey is a fixture at the Ferrari teahouse and enjoys Veronica's company as much as Tim does.

As Starkey passes by, Tim notices a girl walking directly toward him. He hasn't seen her before. *She must be a new student,* he thinks as she approaches. She is cute and has a sweet yet sexy look. Her short brown hair helps accent her brown eyes, light skin, and pleasant looks. She has an equally pleasant figure. "Good morning," she says with a smile that he instantly likes. "Good morning," he replies as she slowly passes by. *Yes, today is a yellow day,* he whispers to himself. "Mike, Mike," he calls out to Mike Campi while he pulls him to the side.

"Mike, who is that girl?"

"That's Joan Simpson. She is a junior. She moved here from Pennsylvania this fall." "Do you know her?"

"Yeah, she is in a couple of my classes."

"She's cute. Is she going with anyone?"

"Not that I know," Mike responds.

Mike Campi is over six feet tall and has a good sense of humor. He enjoys imitating The Three Stooges, is good-natured, and is very observant of people's behavior. He has been attending the Ferrari teahouse parties for several years and can handle himself well in the endless debates that occur when the crew gets together. Despite his size, he hasn't played football mostly because he doesn't want to give up smoking.

The day passes with Tim rushing to get to his hall monitor position in an effort to catch another view of Joan. At the 2:30 break, Joan suddenly appears and slowly approaches him.

"How are you today, Joan?" Tim manages to say as their eyes meet.

"Fine, Tim and you? Looks like we both did our homework," Joan says with a soft voice that turns into a giggle. Their eyes continue to meet.

"This being our second meeting, and you being new to this village, I can introduce you to your new world and give you a tour of this vast two square miles of paradise. Shouldn't we get to know one another?" Tim asks with a smile. Joan smiles, continues to make direct eye contact, and agrees, "Yes, we should."

"How about this Saturday? There's a senior dance this Saturday."

"Sounds good," Joan responds before she hands her phone number to him, while she continues to walk down the hall. *I'm starting to really believe in this yellow day thing,* Tim says to himself. *I wonder where she lives.*

Chapter 6

Too Late for Dessert

Tim heads directly home after football practice. When he enters the house, he smells the strong sent of eggplant Parmesan and knows immediately Veronica is improving. Eggplant Parmesan is one of her best meals and is often saved for special occasions. "Oh, you had a yellow day," Tim sings out as he opens the door. "So did I!"

The kitchen is neatly set for three; Tim, his mother, and father. The smell of the eggplant Parmesan has everyone's attention except Tim's father, Boo. His real name is Bob, but he received the nickname, Boo, when he was young, and it never left him.

Boo has not arrived home yet, and he most likely won't be home anytime soon. It is 5:15 p.m., and dinner is served at 5:30 p.m. at the Ferrari house.

Tim looks at his mother. "Mom, how did you manage to, 'get up,' again?" Tim often uses the expression, "get up," to refer to her recovering from an episode of depression.

"I'm not sure! Maybe it was the new medicine my doctor gave me. Somehow, I feel normal." The depression is gone, and no one knows how long normal will last, but it is clearly time to celebrate.

At 5:30 p.m. Veronica serves the eggplant, and Tim and Veronica sit down and enjoy the meal. Veronica listens to Tim's review of his excellent day, and then outlines all the things she intends to do over the next two weeks. The list is long, and it will take a great deal of time and energy to complete. Tim doesn't question her ability to meet her goals. She is up again and can do anything she sets her mind to when she is normal. Two hours have passed. There is still no sign of Boo. Tim is more concerned about the impact of Boo being late and most likely drunk will have on Veronica's present positive spirit then the amount of work she is planning to do.

Three more hours pass before Tim hears the sound of Boo's car stopping at the front of the house. He goes to the front porch, and he can see that Boo is slumped over the steering wheel and appears to be out cold. He opens the front door of the car and attempts to lift and extract Boo from the car. Boo slowly regains consciousness, "I guess I'm too late for dessert."

"Yeah, I guess so Dad. Mom has gone to bed. There's some leftover eggplant in the fridge."

Boo is a short man with big carpenter's arms and a protruding beer belly. Tim manages to walk Boo into the kitchen, and then leaves him there to fend for himself. Boo, with some difficulty, finds the eggplant and combines it with one more beer before going to bed.

As he enters the bedroom, Veronica addresses him, "Where were you? I prepared your favorite meal. What makes you do this? How could you do this again?"

"I'm no good Veronica. It's my entire fault. I'm just no good, but I'm working on getting better."

His words of admittance calm her outwardly as they always do, but inwardly they always tug at her sense of self-respect and worth to her family. In time, it will lead to another downward spiral.

Boo's life has been one of missed opportunities. When he was a teenager, he worked at the Levy estate taking care of Mrs. Levy's vegetable garden and her German Shepherd dogs. Mrs. Levy took a liking to Boo and wanted to send him to agricultural college since he had a strong interest in gardening. His father told him, "There are enough educated fools in this world. Go out and get a job." Boo followed his father's orders and went to work at a brokerage firm in New York City.

After being passed up several times for a promotion due to the lack of an education, he decided he could make more money as a carpenter and went to work with his father. Mrs. Levy wasn't about to give up on Boo, so she began training him to become a jockey since he was only four feet ten inches tall at the age of nineteen. He excelled in training until he grew five inches at the age of twenty and had to give up his career as a jockey.

Being the president of the local carpenter's union, president of the local Italian American club, and president of the local Royal Arcanum has allowed Boo to demonstrate his leadership skills and has, in a small way, helped compensate for his missed opportunities. Boo has gained the respect of many people in the village. However, his drinking has created problems with his family life. The first ten years of his marriage was during the depression. While his family grew to four children, he spent most of that time living off the charity of others. Like many other men of his day, he first began to drink to ease the pain of not being able to support his family, and then he drank to forget what is was like to be poor, finally he drank out of pure habit. By the time he was working again, he could not break his habit of drinking and had no real intentions of giving it up.

With the excessive drinking and perhaps too much focus on himself, Boo has long ago lost concern for the impact it is having on his wife and family. Although he has never physically hurt Veronica or won't say anything abusive when he gets drunk, the years of being from one hour to three days late have taken their toll.

No one in the family ever admits he is an alcoholic. He simply has a problem. The relationship between Tim and his father has faltered in the years of Veronica's sickness. The two have little to say to one another. Tim blames his father for his mother's condition. When she first was sick, his elder brothers and sister were still living at home, and they would buffer Tim from some of the family stress. Now the family is reduced to three, and Boo's drinking and public drunkenness continues to escalate. The anger Tim feels is kept deep inside. His upbringing does not allow him to express his feelings to his father.

Chapter 7

You Owe It to Yourselves

Saturday Morning begins like any Saturday during football season, a light breakfast, followed by a walk to school, and then suiting up for the game. The team is undefeated. It has won its first four games despite losing most of its starters from the previous year. The previous year, Dobbs Ferry had finished the year undefeated with eight wins and no losses, and no one wants to break the winning streak. Today, they play a home game against Briarcliff.

They are confident that it will be an easy win. However, nothing seems to go right, and by half time, they are losing nineteen to nothing. Coach Bill Brown is silent as they enter the locker room. No one is speaking except Tim. In a low voice, he is giving Starkey a tongue lashing for missing a cross block. When Starkey explains why the play didn't require a cross block, Tim realizes he is the one who made the mistake, and he quickly apologizes to Starkey and remains silent.

Bill Brown is over six feet tall and has a clean-cut look despite his wide build. He is overweight and has a small gut, but he is still a marine from head to toe. He has black straight hair that always looks combed. His commanding voice and self-confidence helps create an authority figure who has gained the respect of the entire football team.

Coach Brown begins his halftime speech slowly. He reminds everyone of the Spartan-like existence they have been living since mid-August. How they had survived the grueling ninety-five degree summer workouts. How they are the only ones who practice past darkness every day. How they have given all they have to give and some how give more in every day of practice.

"My thoughts right now are back in time to the grueling midday heat of August. Back to the punishing workouts and exercises you performed to prepare you for a day like this one. No other team in this league starts practice in midsummer. No other team goes all out like you do during practice. No other team remains on the field until it is dark every night! No other team performs the amount of exercises that we do or goes without water during practice.

"You give it your all because it is in your culture and nature to give your best. You are Dobbs Ferry men. Your school mascot is the same as our nation's. That is not an accident. You are Eagles. You are Dobbs Ferry Eagles, and I am calling on you. You have more to give!"

He doesn't admonish anyone for their poor performance. Instead he treats them like men, and he reaches out to them as if he were speaking to each of them individually.

"I know you have it in you to find that God-given inner strength to turn this game around. You might think you owe it to me to win this game, but you don't. You owe it to yourselves. Many of you never played varsity football until this year. You stood on the sidelines for all those practices and all those years without even a chance to play. Now, you have a chance to prove those years meant something. Some of you have played in previous years, and we are counting on you as leaders of the team. Many of you are seniors and won't be back next year.

"You don't owe me anything. You owe it to yourselves. This is a chance to find out what you are made of. You are a unit—a finely tuned, disciplined, and trained unit. You must all unite in this common cause. This is the most important day of your lives. Except for the day you were born and the day you entered the church, this is the most important day of your lives.

"I would like to take a minute of silence, so you can each reflect on what I am asking of you."

The local villagers make up more than half the team, and they know too well what he is implying. They are not going on to one of the Ivy League schools to become lawyers, doctors, or work in the front office of a prestigious brokerage firm. Many of them aren't even going to college. Some are going to remain in town, working in the trades, or some will attend a two-year college and get a back-office job at one of the local companies. Winning this game will give them local recognition as one of the best comeback teams in Dobbs Ferry football history.

Tim is one of the players who has sat on the sidelines for years, so he is stirred by the coaches comment reminding him of how many beatings he had taken in practice when he was younger only to stand on the sidelines, and how much of his time and energy he has committed to finally be on the starting team. He knows he is about to give beyond whatever he has in him and more.

Each of the players has his own reason to win this game, but despite the coach's words that they don't owe him anything, the entire team's main reason for wanting desperately to win is they simply don't want to let down a man who has shown them respect and treated them as men.

The minute ends and Coach Brown leans back, "What are we?"
"Eagles!" the team roars back.
The coach's voice rises,
"Now go out there as a single united unit!
Unite and win for yourselves!
Unite and prove you are Eagles!
Unite and change your lives forever!"

For a brief moment, there is total silence. Then a deafening roar emanates from the locker room as the team exits with the assistant coaches smacking each one of the players on the head and shoulder as they leave.

Their coach has called upon them to become a single-minded unit, and their Spartan existence has prepared them to respond, but the Briarcliff team has returned to the field determined to maintain its lead. By the end of the third quarter, the score remains nineteen to zero.

Then, in the fourth quarter with time running out, as if someone lit a match, the team ignites and turns into a single unit that would make a Spartan retreat. They score twenty points in the fourth quarter and win the game twenty to nineteen by running for two extra points after scoring a touchdown with seconds on the clock.

It will be a game they will remember the rest of their lives. More importantly, each of them in the future will draw on the experience and find that God-given inner strength needed to withstand real life tragedies and challenges. Tim will be the first one tested, and it will be much sooner than he expects.

Chapter 8

To the Victor Go the Spoils

When an emperor and his army entered Rome after conquering new lands, tradition called for them to be met by throngs of citizens celebrating their glorious victories. After winning a Dobbs Ferry football game, tradition calls for the football players, along with the cheerleaders, to drive their cars down Main Street, while passing motorists honk their horns in celebration of their victory. From the time their cars leave the school parking lot until they reach Main Street, the car horns blare on both sides of the street at a level that no one has ever experienced. Unable to hear one another speak, the victorious group simply waves to all the citizens as they pass.

The victory has struck a cord among the local villagers. Most of the local villagers' parents and older siblings had lost everything during the Great Depression. They know what it is like to lose. More importantly, they know what it takes to continue fighting when you are in the arms of defeat.

At the bar in Sam's Restaurant, a local hangout, many of the older citizens wait to congratulate the conquering heroes. Junior Brogelli, a local, sits with one eye on the window in anticipation of the arrival of the village heroes. A stranger sitting next to him leans over and comments, "I can't help listening in on the conversations. It's clear this village has a real sense of community."

"No question about that!" Junior responds. "And I'll tell you something else. You see that street outside. That's Main Street. You can safely walk down that street at four in the afternoon or four in the morning. And you know why you can do that? Because if someone puts a hand on you at anytime of the day, we will come out and beat the living shit out of them. And if we can't beat the living shit out of them, we'll still beat the living shit out of them." The stranger has just been given a lesson in Dobbs Ferry civic duty, along with being introduced to Dobbs Ferry local logic.

Within minutes, a caravan of cars pulls up to Sam's Pizza, and slowly the village's football team and cheerleaders form a group in front of the restaurant. When they enter the restaurant, everyone at the bar stands up and cheers. While the group is being seated, many of the locals come over to congratulate them on their miraculous win.

Usually the compliments were spread among the quarterback, the backfield, and the receivers. Today, the efforts of the linemen receive equal attention. Everyone basks in the attention and goodwill they receive from the people of the village.

Frank Tulio, one of the starting linemen, stands up and announces, "On behalf of all the linemen, I want everyone to know we are the only guys on the team that are tougher than the women's field hockey team." The crowd laughs. Frank Tulio is a big man with jet-black hair. His easygoing mannerisms and sense of humor disguise the absolute warrior he becomes on the football field.

Just before the pizza is about to be served, Don Sandino, nicknamed Dino, and Nicky Trapiani stand up and ask for everyone's attention. They both feel this victorious day requires a comment from the team leaders.

Dino is an all-around athlete. His neatly combed black hair, attention to dress and charming personality has attracted many girls to him. His confidence and quick thinking abilities make him an excellent speaker. Dino begins, "I will remember this day for the rest of my life. Football more than any other sport I have played in high school requires a team effort. Today Nicky and I are truly honored and lucky to be members of a team in which every player has unselfishly given all he has within him, in one short quarter, to achieve what appeared to be the impossible. I lift my glass to toast you all."

Nicky Trapiani's bright red hair is a gift from his Irish mother. He is six feet tall, weighs 185 pounds, and can run a hundreds yards in 10.1 seconds. Nicky's speed and strength has helped win many games. Nicky lifts his glass, "What else is there to say. Dino has said all that needs to be said. We thank you all for making this a day to remember in Dobbs Ferry High School football and a special day in our lives."

Everyone including the cheerleaders lift their glasses in response. Dino places his arm around his steady girlfriend, Rosanne, while he sips his drink, and then lowers his glass. She has drifted into another world of thought. At about the same time, Tim happens to glance out the restaurant window, where he can see Tito Menetti slowly walking down Main Street.

What a strange guy! Tim thinks as Tito approaches. *He is our age, yet he seldom talks to anyone. He never participates in anything we do and never looks directly at anyone, yet he is somehow forever present.*

"I wonder what that guy thinks about or what he does with his time?" Tim asks Dino as he points to Tito.

"I don't know, and I wouldn't want to find out either," Dino replies with a smile.

Rosanne glances at Dino before looking out the window. Her eyes remain focused on the slow moving figure of Tito as he fades from sight, down the sidewalk of Main Street.

The front door of the restaurant opens, and the stranger leaves thinking what a friendly local crowd and unquestionably safe little village.

Chapter 9

One Night to Remember

Tim arrives at Joan's home at 6:30 on Saturday night. She answers the door after one knock, leaving Tim to believe she was waiting at the door. Their conversation on the way to the school gym is mostly small talk, but somehow Tim finds himself immediately at ease with her. Aside from being cute, she has a great smile and laugh that changes her from cute to sexy.

The school gym and adjacent school cafeteria have been converted to a street in Paris and a Parisian restaurant, compliments of the senior class. Tim helped by drawing a mural of couples dancing that the rest of the decorating committee helped paint and hang on the wall in the gym.

Tim introduces Joan to Dino and his date Rosanne, to Fred and his date Carol Ann and to Starkey and his date Judy. They spend sometime discussing the successful day of football, but as soon as the first fast song begins to play, they head for the dance floor. After a few fast dances, the disc jockey switches to some of the popular slow dances, and Joan and Tim remain on the floor when the first slow dance begins to play.

Perhaps it is the night in Paris atmosphere that comes over them or the simple enjoyment of a young couple coming close together for the first time. They remain together after each slow song, and they continue to dance for sometime after the music has stopped.

"Hey, Romeo and Juliet. Maybe you two want to join the rest of us in the cafeteria for a twenty-minute break?" Dino asks the somewhat overly absorbed couple. When they turn to respond, they realize they are the only ones left on the dance floor, and the music they continue to hear does not come from the Disc Jockey's record player.

Tim and Joan pay little attention to anything said about their attraction to one another. They return to the dance floor after a short break in the cafeteria, saying very little to avoid breaking the spell they are under.

For the first time in a long time, Tim's mind is clear of all other thoughts. He does not stop to think about his mother's present state of mind, or whether his father will make it home sober, or where he might park his car if he is drunk. There is an easy sense of living in the moment that he hasn't experienced since Veronica fell ill. He wants each second to last for an eternity.

When they leave the dancehall, it is late, so Joan asks Tim to drive her directly home. When Tim's car stops in front of her house, all the house lights are out. Joan thanks Tim for the wonderful evening, and they slowly lean toward each other.

He gently kisses her intending to be polite and to make it a short kiss, but somehow it lasts much longer than he intends. She says goodnight with every intention to open the passenger door and leave, but she finds herself returning a tender kiss to him. They remain in the front of the car exchanging kisses for another twenty minutes until Joan realizes it is past 12:00 a.m. *"I'll see you on Monday,"* she whispers to him before she pulls herself away from him, opens the car door, and walks quickly and quietly to her house.

Chapter 10

Fight or Flight

D espite some aches and pains from the previous day's game, Tim wakes up early Sunday morning, gets dressed, and leaves the house by 7:30 a.m. He can use some extra money and is hoping to get in two rounds of eighteen holes (two loops) caddying before the day is done. He arrives at the Ardsley Country Club caddy shack by 7:50 a.m.

He sits on one of the benches alongside the caddy shack where the caddy master, Tony D'Angella, can easily see him. Tony is a tall man with blond curly hair, and a commanding look of a roman soldier that makes it easy to keep most caddies in line. There aren't many caddies available, so Tim is excited about his chances of getting out early. By 8:30 a.m., he still hasn't been assigned any golf bags, he is getting impatient, and many more caddies have arrived. Among them are Marco Devito, Johnny Pacetti, Mike Campi, Bill Moretti, and Peter Reilly. Peter is about fifteen and is short for his age. When Peter gets up for a soda, Marco reaches out. He shoves him down, and kicks him before he lets him up, "You're lucky. I don't charge you for passing by me," he grunts at Peter.

No one ever gets involved in these small demonstrations of aggression. You are expected to fend for yourself in this community. For five years, Marco has been belittling and tormenting caddies that are half his size and strength, so when Bill Moretti, who is six feet tall and weighs over 260 pounds, moves forward, everyone is surprised and happy to see Marco is in trouble.

Bill is a senior at Dobbs Ferry High School. Despite being heavy and having a metal plate in his leg from an auto accident, Bill is extremely agile and has the strength of several men. Although he has inherited his father's black hair, he has a touch of his Irish mother's looks. Bill seldom gets aggressive with anyone. His very size commands respect, and no one in his right mind wants to fight him.

"Marco, come over here. Maybe it's time for you to get some manners," Bill demands. Marco, not wanting to appear frightened and knowing Bill is not likely to fight with him, saunters over to Bill with his fists up, and he throws a left while remaining far enough away, so he can retreat safely if Bill reaches for him.

"You think you are fast enough for this left?" Marco asks Bill staying at what he thinks is a safe distance. As Marco's left hand comes out again, Bill moves at a pace much faster than Marco can imagine, catches Marco's fist in his powerful right hand, and begins to squeeze. Marco cannot free his hand form Bill's viselike grip, and Bill continues to squeeze. A sharp pain emanates from Marco's hand and runs down his arm causing him to sink to his knees.

"I'm losing my patience with you, Marco. You better learn how to behave around here!" Everyone laughs as Marco begs for mercy. Bill releases his grip when Tony, looking at Bill, points to two golf bags, and Bill walks up to the first tee.

With Bill gone, Marco is certain to make someone pay for his embarrassment.

"What are you looking at?" he snaps at Mike Campi.

"What's so funny, Johnny? Wipe that smile off your face," he demands as he grabs Johnny by the neck.

Johnny continues to smile, and Marco backhands him twice. He is about to hit him a third time when an empty wooden coke box slams against his back. Stunned and caught off guard, he turns around.

Holding the coke box in both hands, Tim shouts at him,

"You low life, no good prick! Leave him alone!"

Marco is surprised. He has been rubbing little Tim's nose in the dirt for years. He hasn't looked close enough to see little Tim has gotten bigger, a lot bigger.

"I will let him go, so I can piss on you after I kick the shit out of you."

"The only pissing you're going to do is in your pants, you bonehead!"

As Marco lunges for Tim, Tony grabs him from behind.

"Take this down the back where the members can't see you," Tony demands.

They walk down the back past the parking lot with most of the remaining caddies and Tony following. At the back of the parking lot, there is a twenty-foot flat area followed by a hundred foot long steep embankment. Bushes surround the bottom of the embankment.

When they get to the flat area, Tim, looking very relaxed, asks Marco, "How do you want to do this?" When Marco begins to open his mouth, Tim suddenly hits him with everything he has. Marco doesn't fall. He doesn't even buckle. He just stands there for a second and shakes his head. Not wanting to continue with a fistfight, Tim does the only thing he knows. He tackles Marco, and they roll down to the bottom of the embankment, crashing into the bushes. Marco, in an attempt to quickly get up, somehow catches his head in the bushes.

Tim is on him immediately, slamming him with furious left and right fist and forearm shots. With his head pressed to the ground, Marco is taking a beating. Tim hits him once for all the crap he has taken from him in past years. He hits him again for all the other smaller guys that have taken his crap. He hits him for picking on defenseless Johnny. He hits him for being a prick and then continues in a seemingly endless flailing of fists and forearm shots.

Marco appears to be going out, so Tim gets up and starts kicking him in the side. He kicks him because the world is full of heartless bastards like Marco. He kicks him to make Marco suffer the same way he has made others suffer.

"Get him off him!" Tony shouts realizing this one is going too far. The next thing Tim knows he is being pulled away from Marco by several of the other caddies, but not before he gets one good punch to the groin not unlike what he used to receive from Marco. Amazingly Marco gets up after they back Tim away. Tony stands in front of Marco.

"You have had enough, Marco. Go home and clean up," Tony demands.

"I'm not done with him!"

The crowd that has gathered to bet on the fight loudly laughs.

At about this time, blood begins to come out of his nose, mouth, and one of his ears. Marco reaches his hand to his face, and it fills with blood. The big tough guy turns a bit white and flashes a look of fear.

"It's coming out of your ear too, and who knows where else," Tony says with a big grin.

The crowd laughs again.

"It's time to go home, Marco."

Acting like he's being forced to leave, Marco responds, "Okay I'll go. I want to see you Wednesday behind the Grand Union, Ferrari, so we can finish this."

"I'll be waiting for you, meathead!" Tim replies.

Marco backs up, turns around, and leaves the premises as fast as his aching and swollen body can carry him. The rest of the smaller caddies who have remained safely at the top of the embankment begin cheering and come racing down to Tim. Marco has finally gotten the beating he deserves by someone smaller than him. In an expression of pure elation, they lift Tim up and carry him back on their shoulders to the caddy shack. No one could see from the top of the embankment that Marco had his head caught in the bushes, and Tim isn't about to tell them. Moreover, Tim isn't about to tell them when Marco was able to lift himself up, he was shaking inside and was closer to flight than fight.

Chapter 11

The Great Escape

On Monday morning, when Tim begins to wake up, he can hear the sounds of his mother singing. She is in the kitchen preparing breakfast, and she has already cleaned half the house. He puts on a green shirt. It is obviously an Irish morning. Veronica not only has breakfast ready, but she is cutting up vegetables for a vat of her best homemade soup, clam chowder.

"Is it a clam chowder night?" Tim asks as he enters the kitchen.

"Enough for an army!" she responds.

Veronica's Manhattan clam chowder is not only a family favorite, but it usually attracts most of Tim's friends.

Tim, content in knowing his mother is up again, eats his breakfast and heads for the front door. He is running a little late, and he doesn't want to waste anytime getting to school. He opens the front door and looks out on the front porch expecting to see his dog, Daisy, waiting for him. Daisy, a collie mix, is an intelligent and obedient dog. She waits for Tim every morning before he leaves for school. She is not on the porch. He leans back into the house.

"Mom, is Daisy somewhere in the house?"

"No! I let her out, so she can say good-bye to you as she does every morning."

"Well, she is not here," Tim says with some alarm in his voice.

Tim's early morning routine of checking on Daisy and making sure she is in the house before he leaves has existed for years. Six years ago, she was run over by a car after following him to school. She survived the accident, and for six years, Tim has held a vigilant watch to make sure it doesn't happen again.

"I'm going to go see if I can find her. She's not here now."

"Don't worry, Tim. She's been spending her mornings with the new neighbor's dog for the last week. I'll go over and pick her up in a little while."

"Thanks, Mom. You know how I am about her."

Veronica's words have reduced his fear of a potential problem enough for him to continue on his morning route to school, and he moves at a fast pace to avoid being late.

On the other side of the village, in the river park not far from the railroad tracks, Marco Devito can be seen walking a dog. The dog, on a long leash, is struggling, while it is being dragged along. It is Daisy.

"Marco, I see you have a gift for me," Tito calls out. When they are only a few feet from the railroad tracks, Daisy begins to growl at the sight of Tito. It is as though she can see the evil within her executioner.

Holding the rope he will use to tie her head to the track in one hand, Tito reaches out with his other hand to calm her. Daisy, who has never acted aggressive to a human, lunges forward, jumps into the air, and bites the hand that is about to kill her. Marco pulls back on the leash, but it is too long to stop Daisy's attack. Tito pulls his hand back. By now,

Daisy has sunk her teeth in deep. Tito begins to run in the opposite direction of Marco in an attempt to free himself of Daisy's grip. Marco holds tightly to the leash. Somehow, the force of the two pulling in opposite directions causes the collar on Daisy's neck to snap, freeing her from Marco's leash and causing Tito to fall forward into the dirt.

Daisy, sensing she is free of the leash, lets go of Tito's gnarled and bleeding hand, and runs across the railroad tracks toward the woods, where safety awaits. Tito, with his one good hand, reaches into his pocket and pulls out his pellet gun. He had planned to use the pellet gun to knock her out before he tied her to the track. Now he is using it to stop her escape. Being tied to the railroad track would be an easy way to die compared to what he will do if he catches her.

As Daisy jumps over the third rail of the tracks, Tito, having lined up the sites of the gun on her, squeezes the trigger. The pellet hits the back of her left hind leg as she clears the third rail, and tumbles onto the ground. The throbbing pain in her leg temporarily paralyzes her. Tito has lined the sites of the gun up on her again and fires another shot. It misses her. A moment later, she recovers from the shock of being shot and disappears into the woods.

Chapter 12

Veronica's Vultures

Tim arrives at home by 5:30 p.m. realizing that Veronica's clam chowder may attract a crowd. Veronica meets him at the door.

"Tim, I have looked all over the neighborhood. Daisy wasn't at the neighbor's house. I have walked to school and back twice searching for her. I should have let you look for her this morning!"

"Mom, it's not your fault if she decided to wander away. It's not the first time she has done this. She will find her way home. Anyway, it's dark out now, so there isn't much we can do."

Tim's response is more out of concern for his mother's state of mind than his concern for his dog. "When Dad gets home, I'll take a quick ride around the village to see if I can spot her. Until then, let's have some of your clam chowder. It should help calm our nerves."

As Tim steps inside the house, he is not surprised to find that Starkey, Mike Campi, and Freddie Kerry have stopped by to say hello to Veronica. Obviously the word has gotten out that Veronica's teahouse is open for business.

Tim is happy to see Fred Kerry has joined the crew. He hasn't seen much of Fred since he started dating his new girlfriend Carol Ann. Veronica has watched this same group of boys make plans over her kitchen table for everything from go-cart races to restoring an old boat that sank in the Hudson River on its first voyage. They narrowly escaped drowning when the new explorers were rescued by a passing friend's boat.

"We just stopped by for a little tea," Starkey explains to Tim with a smile. When Tim enters the kitchen, he can see that Veronica has already made a pot of tea and set the teacups out for his friends.

As members of the Ferrari teahouse, over the years they have sampled most of her cooking, and her clam chowder is the crowd's favorite soup. If the word gets out she is cooking up a vat, it will be spread around the neighborhood in a matter of hours. *Someone must have stopped by earlier for these guys to be here so soon,* Tim thinks while looking at the crew that has already arrived.

"We hear Daisy is missing," Freddie says while they all sit down at the kitchen table.

"Is there anything we can do to help?"

"You can join me when Boo comes home. I'm going to use his car to see if I can spot her tonight."

"Well, if you're all going to be waiting for Boo, you might as well join us for dinner. I have made some clam chowder, and it's ready to serve," Veronica explains.

"That's not necessary. Maybe we'll have one small bowl to clear our heads on what to do to help find Daisy," Freddie responds.

Veronica waits until the boys finish their first cup of tea Then she prepares a large bowl of soup for each of the boys. She always uses the fresh vegetables she buys from Roxie's vegetable truck. She has her own hand vegetable grinder that she uses to make the juice that she adds to the soup, along with freshly caught clams from the fish market. Somehow, she is able to repeat the same flavorful soup every time she makes it. The broth is hearty, but it doesn't overtake the taste of the clams. While you can easily taste the clams, the flavors of each vegetable and the potatoes are not lost in the soup. A single spoon of the soup bursts with a variety of flavors, yet it doesn't settle heavy in your stomach. At the completion of a single bowl, a young man will have plenty of room for more.

"Oh Tim, Bill Moretti came by this afternoon. He mentioned you had a fight with someone at the golf course, and he wants to hear more about what happened. I hope no one got hurt. I told him he would have to come by later, and you wouldn't be home until after football practice."

At that moment, Bill Moretti walks through the front door.

"Bill, come in. Help yourself to some clam chowder."

"I'll get that for him, Mrs. Ferrari," Starkey says making his way to the vat with his empty bowl. Starkey fills a bowl of soup for Bill, and then refills his own bowl, as well as Freddie's, Mike's, and Tim's. No one objects.

They have all finished their third bowl of soup when Mary Jane Dowling and Carl Denato enter the house. They are friends of Tim's sister Jane Ferrari, and although Jane is attending nursing school, they still frequently stop by to visit Veronica. After filling a bowl of soup for his most recent guests, Tim realizes there is only enough left to fill another bowl, so he finishes off the remaining clam chowder.

Within minutes, Boo's car pulls up in front of the house, and everyone, having decided to help search for Daisy, piles into Boo's car. Boo enters the house a mere two hours late. *Ah! The smell of Veronica's clam chowder,* he thinks as he enters the kitchen. Veronica has already gone upstairs to bed. From down in the kitchen comes a scream.

"Those vultures have eaten all of the clam chowder."

Chapter 13

A Birthday Party

T im slowly drives by a number of places that Daisy likes to visit. The search group has several flashlights, and they do their best to shine their lights in every direction when they pass each site. The boys spend time searching the village parks, the woods that surround Mohican Park Avenue, and the ponds around the golf course; all areas that Daisy has spent time with Tim in the past five years, but there was no sign of her. By 10:00 p.m., they decide to head home, but first, they will stop at Vels, one of the village's local pubs located at the bottom of Main Street. Bill mentioned it is Nicky Trapiani's birthday, and he probably will be celebrating at Vels. When they enter Vels, Nicky is sitting at the bar with Dino, and they are both drinking a coke.

"Hey, you guys come on in and celebrate with me. It's my birthday today!" exclaims Nicky.

Bill sits down next to them, "Looks like the football captains are setting an example. No beers for them during the football season," Bill announces.

The bartender pours eight beers and leans over the bar, "Okay, it's time to celebrate and one beer isn't going to end anyone's football career."

After a short pause, everyone lifts a beer, and the bartender toasts Nicky a happy birthday. They all drink their beer despite the fact that Nicky and Tim are the only ones who are eighteen.

"You guys all got together for me. I appreciate you all being here, especially since it's a little late for a football season night," Nicky says to the crew.

"We were on an earlier mission to find Tim's dog Daisy," Bill confesses.

Nicky's eyes light up, "A funny thing happened today. I drove down to the river to relax, and a pack of about seven or eight stray dogs were mulling around the dump. Scrounging for food, I guess! One of them looked just like Daisy. She was limping, and it looked like they were following her. It couldn't be her. I tried to get a closer look, and she growled and snarled as though she was about to attack me."

Chapter 14

In An Italian Mood

By Wednesday, Tim has searched just about every conceivable place in Dobbs Ferry's two square miles but to no avail. When Daisy was only two years old, she had jumped out of Boo's car. They were over three miles from home and she had found her way home within two days, so Tim is certain she will find her way home if she is not in an accident. Since there were no reports of her being hit by a car, there is still a chance she will be home soon.

On Wednesday morning, Tim is up and out of the house early. He is wearing a bright red shirt, green pants, and white socks to honor the Italian flag since he is in an Italian mood. His ancestors on the Italian side of the family represent the business side of the family. They are mostly small businessmen and own hunting lodges, Italian restaurants, delicatessens, etc. throughout New York State. They are industrious, bright, and the most successful side of his family. However, Tim knows very little about them other than a small amount of information he picks up at funerals when one of his Italian cousins attends.

Veronica had first learned how to cook Italian meals from his grandma Ferrari, who in turn had learned from her brothers Joseph and Louis. They arrived in Dobbs Ferry, New York, after their mother, Tim's great-grandmother, sent them a letter telling them they must sell their businesses in Peru and go to America. Their sister Catherine was living in sin by dating an American sailor.

The two brothers sold their businesses in Peru and sailed immediately to New York to find their sister and end this dreadful relationship. They arrived in New York two years later due to the slow pace of the freighter ship they had boarded in Peru in 1896. They sent a letter back to their mother, who was living in Genoa, Italy, informing her that they had located Catherine, but they realized they were at least one year late when a little girl, Tim's aunt Gertrude, opened the door to their sister Catherine's house. The two brothers became chefs at Delmonicos, a famous Italian restaurant in downtown New York City and settled in Long Island, New York.

Tim takes great pride in both his Irish and Italian background. His Irish relatives are mostly railroad men. They helped build and maintain the New York Hudson railroad for the past hundred years. His Italian relatives' ability to travel throughout the world, their skills as small business people, their cooking talents, and their unwavering commitment to their family are admirable family traits that he finds appealing and wants to emulate.

During the Depression, many of the families in the village helped one another to survive. Boo was without a means of making a living. An Italian family, the Pasanos, had welcomed the Ferrari family into their home until Boo was able to get work again. Veronica's skills in cooking Italian meals further improved during this time. Although Veronica's knowledge of Italian cooking is not as diverse as those of an Italian housewife, her Italian sauces and a half dozen of her Italian dishes are exceptionally good. She loves to cook, and she is an excellent student. Her Italian meals are always light on the stomach but strong in flavor with excellent sauces. Her blend of Italian, Irish, and American food makes for a steady flow of excellent meals that Tim and the rest of the family thoroughly enjoy.

Tim leaves school a little early, so he can be at the back of the Grand Union by 3:00 p.m., the time Marco set for their next confrontation. He arrives at the Grand Union at 3:00 p.m., and by 3:30 p.m., it is clear that Marco is not going to show. Bullies are cowards and seldom want to fight anyone who is not afraid to fight. They prey only on the weak, and on those that are not likely to fight back. Marco is a coward, and now, he has shown his true colors.

Before going home, Tim enters the Grand Union to buy the list of ingredients Veronica has given him, so they can make meatballs and spaghetti for dinner. While wandering the aisles and filling his cart with meats, cheese, and bread, he turns a corner and just misses running into Joan Simpson. He has been thinking about her on and off for the past five days, but football practice and his lost dog has kept him busy. The few times she had passed him in the hall, they exchanged long smiling glances and hellos, but they weren't able to talk.

Joan taps his shopping cart.

"Well, where have you been hiding?"

Tim moves close to her, "I had some personal business to attend to this week."

Joan moves as close as she can get to him without touching,

"Do you think you can find sometime for me this week?"

"Of course, I can. In fact, I'm going home to help make dinner with my mom. Do you want to join me?"

"Yes, I would. I would like to meet your parents."

After they exit the Grand Union, Joan puts her arm around Tim's free arm and leans on him, while they walk up Ashford Avenue. Now that he has invited her home, Tim's first thoughts are how do I introduce her to Boo. Chances are Boo isn't home yet, and if he is home, hopefully, he isn't drunk. Veronica has been up and running for a few days. This morning she was fine, so he doesn't have to worry about her being depressed.

Across the street from the Grand Union, out of view of the closely attached couple, Marco is pointing to Tim and gesturing, while Tito listens.

"I have done many favors for you, Tito. I want a favor from you. I want you to teach him a lesson. Make him feel some real pain. Break his arms or something like that."

Tito has stopped listening to Marco. His attention is drawn to Joan. He finds her attractive and wants to see more of her. "If you want to hurt him that badly, Marco, why don't you do it yourself?" Tito begins to walk in the direction of the couple, leaving Marco behind. After a block, he stops. They are heading too far from Main Street. He is uncomfortable being more than a few blocks from Main Street.

When they arrive home, Veronica is already in the kitchen and getting ready for him. The necessary pots, pans, and spices are on the kitchen stove.

"Mom, I would like you to meet Joan Simpson."

They both smile and exchange greetings.

Tim leans over the big cooking pot, "Have you ever made meatballs and spaghetti, Joan?"

"Yes, of course."

"Well, we're going to show you how to cook it Italian style," responds Tim. "We will start by making a base for the sauce. We need to pour a small amount of this olive oil into this pot and heat it up. While it is heating, we have to chop up these onions and garlic. To help make the sauce light tasting, we have to fry the tomato paste in a frying pan with a little oil and garlic to get the acidic taste out of the paste. The pork will add flavor to the sauce. When the olive oil is heated, we will add the garlic and onions to the pot, and let them brown. Then we'll add the fried tomato paste, and finally, a little wine to create the base for the sauce. When the base is complete, we will add the chopped tomatoes, pork, spices, and meatballs."

Joan leans back for a second, "You are a man of many talents, aren't you!"

Tim smiles, not mentioning that this is the only meal he knows how to prepare. While Joan and Tim prepare the sauce, Veronica creates the meatballs. When the meatballs are ready, they are fried in oil and garlic, and then they are gently dropped into the sauce. They let the sauce simmer for another hour and a half.

By six o'clock, the meal is ready. Joan has called her parents to let them know she is eating at Tim's house, and they sit down to an enjoyable meal. Joan begins to eat and stops, "Mrs. Ferrari, these meatballs are delicious, and the sauce is excellent, Tim." Throughout dinner, Tim is worried that Boo will come charging through the front door drunk. When they finish eating, Veronica asks Joan if she wants a freshly baked piece of apple pie for dessert.

Joan thanks her for the offer, but tells her she must get home soon. She has to study for an exam tonight. Tim is relieved. He offers to walk her home, and she accepts.

"I'm having the girls by for bridge tonight at 8:30. Can you bring back a quart of milk?" Veronica asks Tim before he leaves. Having the girls over for bridge is a sure sign that she has fully recovered from her last depression.

The fall night air is cool. Joan and Tim walk at a brisk pace while clinging tightly together, unaware the steely eyes of Tito Menetti are closely watching them, again, as they walk toward the village.

Tito follows the couple until they pass Cedar Street, and they continue up Broadway toward Villard Hill where Joan lives. Villard Hill is a section of the village where the more affluent families live, and Tito never travels beyond his comfort zone.

His growing need to dominate is making him tense and frustrated. His rape of Rosanne was spontaneous. He had not planned it, and yet he has gotten away with it. He is confident if he plans his next conquest, it will last longer, and he will continue to go undetected. Although Joan appears to be of interest to him, she lives on Villard Hill, and she is not likely to use the aqueduct to go to school. In fact, he has never seen her walking the aqueduct.

Tito turns toward Main Street. He decides to go home. He becomes engrossed in thoughts of his next conquest, and he is unaware that he is being followed. Rosanne has been tracking him all night. Out of fear, she remains at a safe distance. Out of anger and rage, she has been tracking him for days. She wants to know when and where he goes. She wants to know when and where he is most vulnerable.

When Tim arrives back home, Veronica's bridge group are gathered around the kitchen table and have already started to play. The same group of Irish women has been playing bridge since Tim was a baby. They spend most of their time chatting about what is going on in the village and their families. In between the chatting and drinking tea, they manage to play a round or two of bridge.

Tim places the milk he bought for their tea in the refrigerator, says hello to everyone, and walks over to the door that separates the kitchen from the dining room, where he can go through a routine that he has been performing for the bridge group since he was ten. It has become a bridge club tradition.

His goal is to make them laugh. Their goal is to do their best to ignore him and most importantly not to laugh. When he was younger, everyone would laugh at his antics until one night he was able to climb the walls of the downstairs foyer. He wet his feet and hands, so they would stick to the plaster walls in the narrow hallway, and then he simply climbed up the walls to the ceiling. It is a trick that his sister Jane taught him when they were small. When the bridge group entered the house, they were greeted by Tim stretched out on the ceiling above them. They had to walk under him to get to the kitchen. Veronica asked the group not to pay attention to him or laugh at him anymore to avoid encouraging him.

Tim's first move is to stand on the other side of the doorway and wraps one arm back and around his head and grab his chin to make it look like someone is attacking him from behind. It's a simple and old trick, but sometimes, it gets someone to laugh. No one falls for it.

He decides to do a switch up and walks to the other end of the kitchen, opens the cellar door, and walks onto the top of the cellar steps, where there are a number of metal items hanging above the stairs. He drops a metal cleaning bucket down the stairs and screams for help at the same time. He can't hear anyone laughing on the other side of the cellar door, so he opens the cellar door and returns to the doorway between the kitchen and the dining room.

Still not discouraged, he moves to the dining room side of the doorway. Then he walks past the door with one bent arm in front and one bent arm behind him imitating an Egyptian walking. One of the women laughs. "Good night, ladies," Tim says and retreats upstairs to his bedroom. He can see from the corner of his eye that while Veronica is ignoring him, she has a big smile on her face.

Chapter 15

A New Day

Sunday morning has arrived too soon. As usual, Tim is still sore from Saturday's game. There aren't many chances to caddy in the fall, so he gets up early and heads for the golf course. He arrives at the caddy shack a little after 7:00 a.m. It is the first time he has returned since his fight with Marco. Many of the regulars are already seated on the benches along the fence. Marco is nowhere to be seen.

Tim sits down next to Father John. He enjoys listening to some of Father John's philosophy on life. It always makes the wait go faster. Father John's real name is John Cleary. He received the nickname Father John because he constantly uses the phrase, "bless you," as he makes the sign of the cross. The black shirts he likes to wear and his innocent-looking Irish face topped with white hair add to the priestly image.

Father John, along with several of the older caddies, is a WWII veteran. Bob Cirillo, known as Blackie because of his jet-black hair, and Father John both survived D-Day and the Battle of the Bulge. They are both in their early forties, yet they look more like they are sixty years old. The war had taken its toll on them, along with the endless amount of alcohol they have consumed in an attempt to forget what they had witnessed and endured.

Before Tim has a chance to say hello to Father John, three of the older caddies, including Blackie, who witnessed last week's fight, shake Tim's hand, and they compliment him for a job well done and for protecting defenseless Johnny.

Blackie, a small man, weighs 130 pounds soaking wet. He likes to roll his cigarette pack up in his shirtsleeve, a practice left over from his army days. He always stands as tall as his five-foot five-inch frame allows him when addressing someone. He looks you straight in the eye when he is speaking to you. Despite his small size, he creates an overall appearance of someone you wouldn't want to upset. When Blackie shakes Tim's hand, Tim, for the first time, can't help noticing, despite all the bravado, there is sadness in Blackie's eyes. Tim had seen that same sadness in a picture of his great-grandfather who had survived the Civil War.

Blackie had landed on Normandy Beach on D-Day. He fought his way through France, into Germany, and continued fighting until the Germans surrendered. Fifteen years of alcohol and a horrifying war experience has not completely removed the look of a man ready for combat.

Tim looks directly at Blackie when he shakes his hand. "I am happy to have gained your respect, Blackie," Tim says with conviction. Most of the young people of the village are grateful for what the men of WWII did to protect our country, and they treat the vets with respect regardless of their present condition.

"Victory can be both sweet but short at the same time, so savor the brief moments of joy," Father John whispers low enough for only Tim to hear.

"You appeared to be fearless in facing a much bigger opponent, and you were fighting for a defenseless soul. You are truly a noble caddie with a shining yellow Coca-Cola box. Bless you, sir Tim."

"I was close to running away most of the fight. I somehow turned the fear into aggression," Tim explains.

"Fear consumes most of us when threatened. It's how you react to the fear that counts," responds Father John.

Tim wants to ask if fear had gripped Father John in the midst of a battle, but he stops short of asking. There is an unwritten rule when talking to a WWII vet. Don't ask any direct questions about the war. Most vets don't want to be reminded of the war. If they happen to offer up some information, then you can kick back and take in the story, but you never ask direct questions.

"Fight or flight! When do you know what is the right thing to do?" Tim asks attempting to avoid a direct question about the war.

"You fight to protect yourself and those closest to you. Flight should only happen if there are no other options remaining, or no one is left to protect but you. It would be better to die protecting those closest to you than retreat only to watch them be destroyed," explains Father John.

Tim has touched a raw nerve and realizes that his question was too close to the war. "Thank you, Father John for the words of wisdom. Now, when is Tony going to let us out on a loop?"

"Soon, he is a busy man, God bless him."

Starkey had arrived a few minutes after Tim, and he, too, is getting impatient. He decides to get a snack and goes up to the caddy shack window, where there are miniature blueberry pies lining a shelf, just inside the building. He has his money to pay for the pie, but no one is at the window, so he places some money on the shelf and takes one blueberry pie. As he turns to return to his seat, the assistant pro golfer, Brad Waldelton, snaps a towel at Starkey that he had been using to clean golf clubs and catches Starkey in the neck. Starkey cringes with pain. "Don't you ever take anything off these shelves without my permission," he barks at Starkey.

Starkey goes back to his seat and slowly removes the wrapping paper from the pie. When he is done, he gets up and returns to the caddy shack window.

"Brad, can I speak with you for a minute?" he asks.

"If you have any questions or complaints, you can start by moving away from the window," Brad demands as he stands up and walks toward Starkey. His immaculate dress consisting of a bright green golf shirt, well-pressed golf pants, and polished golf shoes are meant not only to impress the members but also to show class distinction and authority over the caddies.

Starkey is not impressed with his clothes or his position at the country club. All he knows is some asshole just caused him a great deal of pain. Before Brad can reach the window, Starkey flings his blueberry pie, hitting Brad in the center of his chest and splattering over the rest of his clothes. Brad grabs the nearest golf club and climbs out the window. Starkey is already halfway up the first fairway by the time Brad is out the window.

"Enjoy your pie, Brad," he yells. "It's a gift. You don't have to pay for it."

"You'll never caddy here again!"

"Who gives a shit? I'll be off to college next year, and you'll still be sitting around here kissing ass and cleaning the members' clubs."

Tony is suddenly visible at the corner of the caddie shack. "Tim, you and your buddy Johnny, take these bags." Tony commands. "The Andersons and the Stewarts will tee off in five minutes."

Tim ignores the connection Tony makes between him and Johnny and moves quickly to make sure he gets the Stewart's bags. Mr. Stewart can be a little demanding of his caddy, and Tim doesn't want Johnny to be subjected to Stewart's fury if Johnny commits an infraction of the rules.

Johnny goes ahead up the first fairway before the members tee off, so he can watch where each ball lands to avoid any lost balls. Tim notices someone come out of the woods, appears to have a brief conversation with Johnny, and then disappears into the woods. When all the members finish driving the ball, Tim catches up with Johnny. "Who was that person that came out of the woods?" Tim asks.

"It was Tito Menetti," Johnny answers.

"What does he want?"

"He wants half my money when I finish caddying," Johnny responds with a look of fear.

Tim's effort to keep Johnny out of Mr. Stewart's way fails when Johnny decides to attend the flagstick on the first hole and allows his shadow to block the line of Mr. Stewart's ball.

"Listen Son, if you don't know what you're doing, you shouldn't be out here," Stewart growls at Johnny. "Your shadow is blocking my line of sight!" Johnny looks confused, so Tim tells Johnny to go ahead to the next hole, while he attends the flagstick.

It seems Johnny has to take it from everyone, even from those who should know better. If he makes it through the eighteen holes, he will be lucky to get a decent tip from such upper-crust goons. If he manages to get home without Tito or Marco taking his money, he will probably have to give what he has earned to his mother. Yet despite what the day brings, he will end it with a smile.

When Tim catches up with Johnny on the next hole, he can see Johnny is looking a little confused and concerned about what just happened. "Listen, Johnny, it may not seem like it right now, but today is going to be a good day."

"How do you know that, Tim?" Johnny asks.

"Because I'm wearing a yellow shirt and a yellow belt today. When I wear yellow, it's almost always a good day. If we see something unusual out here, it will be proof it's a good day."

"Today's a yellow day," Johnny repeats as he continues walking up the second fairway.

A loop on the Ardsley Country Club golf course is a trip down memory lane for Tim. To get to the second hole, you must cross Route 9, which runs north to the village of Irvington.

An old house that has been vacant for years faces Route 9 just before you get to the second hole. Tim and several friends, a few years back, had managed to enter it through an unlocked window. The house was empty, but Tim found a New York newspaper in mint condition dated 1881 and a shoe brush in the attic. They returned a week later after deciding to make it a clubhouse only to find the second floor had collapsed onto the first floor.

The second hole through the fifth hole is all on a huge flat rectangular track of land. It is a dividing line between the middle class and the rich. The south and west sides of the golf course are surrounded by middle-class homes. The north and east sides are surrounded by large, expensive homes with well-manicured lawns and shrubbery. The sixth through the eighteenth hole is a richly wooded area where the wealthiest residents live.

On the left side of the sixth hole is the duck pond, where Tim has spent many mornings fishing when he was younger. On the right side of the sixth hole is a dirt road that is partly blocked from view by shrubs that line the sixth fairway and is one of his favorite places to take a date at night. You can drive your car up the dirt road, where it is hidden from view, and then it is a short walk to the sixth fairway, where you can make out under the stars.

The seventh hole is where Starkey would often help his favorite member, Mr. Flynn, out of one of the course's most difficult traps by throwing a golf ball up onto the green after Mr. Flynn would swing his sand wedge to make it look like he had hit the ball out of the trap. Despite not being a very good player, he would bet heavily on each round of golf. Starkey would do his best to help him from losing and would get an excellent tip in return.

Alongside the eighth fairway is Mr. and Mrs. Green's mini estate. Tim and Peter Brogelli had maintained the Greens' yard a few years back. Peter has joined the marines, so Tim doesn't get to see him anymore. Peter is a tough kid with a big heart, and Tim misses working with him. The ninth fairway is flooded with water in the winter, making it a great place to ice skate most of the winter. When Tim was thirteen, he took his first date skating on the ninth fairway.

Woods surround the ninth hole through the fourteenth hole. The few existing mansions along these holes are set back in the woods, creating an area that seems lost in time and giving you a sense of what the Native Americans experienced when they lived on this land. Behind the thirteenth hole, Tim's Boy Scout troop, on several occasions, had hiked through the woods and slept overnight.

On the fifteenth hole is an old barn used by a tree surgery company to store their trucks. When he was thirteen, Tim and several friends had snuck into the barn and uncovered the contents of an entire home from the 1920s stored in the attic. They agreed not to remove any of the items from the attic and turned it into a meeting place for their newly formed club until the owner realized it was being used.

To the right of the fifteenth fairway are woods that lead to the Belsuva estate. The estate has a huge pond that is teeming with large bass, mostly because few people ever fish there. The reason few people fish the pond is the caretaker will shoot rock salt at you if he catches you on the property. Tim and Peter Brogelli have fished at the pond numerous times in the early morning before the caretaker arrives. Once they even placed the fish in buckets filled with water and carried them across the golf course down to the

Green's house and stocked their small pond with the bass. There aren't many places around the golf course that Tim and his friends haven't ventured into when he was younger. The members of the country club may think they have the only rights and privileges to the golf course, but they have been sharing the use of the area for years, and most of them don't know it.

By the time the Andersons and Stewarts have completed the fourteenth hole, the day has been somewhat uneventful. The fifteenth hole is Tim's favorite hole. It is a long par five hole and has a cliff like drop about 250 yards from the tee. Most players drive to the top of the cliff then, instead of trying to hit the second shot to the green, they hit a short iron that positions them in front of a small pond that surrounds most of the green. The beautiful view from the top of the cliff looking down on the pond and the green is what makes the fifteenth hole the golf club's signature hole.

Mr. Anderson tees up a ball and hits a solid shot down the center of the fairway about ten yards short off the top of the cliff. "No matter how many times I play this hole, this view is always breathtaking," he explains as he approaches his ball. His second shot lands directly in front of the pond. When they reach the bottom of the hill, Johnny hands Mr.

Anderson his nine iron. If he can put his nine iron shot on the green, he will have a chance at a birdie. He swings and makes solid contact with the ball. As he completes his swing, Johnny points back to the top of the cliff. "Look up, there," Johnny utters loud enough for everyone to hear. They all turn in time to see three deer, with large antlers, standing at the top of the cliff in the center of the fairway. It is a breathtaking sight. Mr. Anderson turns his head back in the direction of the hole in time to see his ball drop into the hole.

"An eagle! I just got an eagle! I have never eagled this hole. I can't believe it. A beautiful view of nature followed by an eagle! What a great moment! What a day!" Mr. Anderson shouts.

"You'll have to keep that ball to remind you of the occasion," Tim says to Mr. Anderson as he glances at Johnny and smiles.

"Yes, I believe I will," responds Mr. Anderson, "In fact, I am going to have that ball encased in a clear plastic box and keep it on my desk at work to remind me of this day."

When they complete the round of golf, Mr. Anderson hands Johnny ten dollars instead the usual tip of seven dollars. "Thank you, Johnny. That was truly a golf moment on the fifteenth hole I will remember for a long time."

"You have to believe in the power of yellow," Tim reminds Johnny before he leaves.

"Today was a yellow day," Johnny responds with a big smile.

On Johnny's way home from caddying, Tito stops him and relieves him of five of the dollars he just earned.

Chapter 16

The Induction

After finishing his loop, Tim returns home as quickly as he can. He has tests on Monday and plans to spend the rest of the day, studying. When he gets to the front door of his house, he is surprised to find Boo waiting for him.

"Get changed and ready as fast as you can," Boo demands. "This afternoon is Father-Son-Day at the Royal Arcanum, and we're going to be late if you don't hurry up."

Boo had never informed Tim of the event, but Tim does not object. It would be foolish to object. It looks like schoolwork will have to wait for now.

Tim has never been to a Father-Son-Day at the Royal Arcanum. In fact, he has never heard of the event before.

The Royal Arcanum is a men's fraternity organization not unlike the Knights of Columbus. It differs, however, in that its membership includes Catholics, Jews, and Protestants. Louie Miller, the owner of a local hardware store, and Boo have been taking turns as president of the local chapter for years. Although the villagers mingle with one another at village events, for the most part they remain segregated when joining clubs or fraternal organizations.

The Royal Arcanum is founded on the principles of good citizenship. It promotes love of country, home and friends, the fatherhood of God and brotherhood of man, faithfulness in performance of obligations of the home, honor in your dealings with mankind, generosity with those less fortunate than yourself, sympathy, kindness and consideration for the bereaved and distressed. One of its objectives is to teach morality without religious distinction, patriotism without partisanship, and brotherhood without creed or class. You have to admire all of the members for taking a leap across the invisible boundaries that religion and money too often create.

Louie Miller and Boo have worked tirelessly over the years to increase the membership and to get small benefits, such as life insurance for the members. Both Louie and Boo have difficulty hearing, so when they are on the phone, they speak loud enough for Tim to hear both their conversations. Louie is a religious man, and his commitment to helping others and to support his community is a reflection of his Jewish faith. He always looks and acts like he is on a mission, and you are welcome to join him. Tim believes Louie has a positive effect on Boo and is always glad to see them get together.

Boo's membership in this club has always intrigued Tim. When Tim and Boo arrive at the Royal Arcanum hall, Boo quickly disappears into the background, while three men dressed in colorful robes surround Tim. Each robe has a word printed on it. One says Charity, another says Honor, and still another says Brotherhood.

"Tim, today is your induction ceremony into the Royal Arcanum," the Brotherhood member announces. Mr. Brotherhood continues with a five-minute speech on the brotherhood of man and consideration for the bereaved and distressed. Mr. Honor steps forward next and lectures Tim on his obligation to honor his country, home, and friends.

Finally, Mr. Charity steps forward and Tim realizes he is Martin Levy. Martin works for his father at the local cigar store. While Martin is reasonably intelligent, he has a speech impediment and sounds a bit like Elmer Fudd when he speaks. Martin begins, "Chawaty. One must be Chawatable" Tim bites his cheeks to avoid in laughing, but he cannot hold back and breaks out in laughter. He tries to avoid embarrassing Martin by apologizing and explaining that seeing him in this fifteenth century robe is making him laugh.

Martin continues without accepting his apology, and Tim realizes Martin knows why he was laughing as well as the fifty members that are quietly standing behind him.

When the ceremony is over, every member shakes Tim's hand and congratulates him. Tim doesn't feel like celebrating. He can't help thinking Martin, who has had to deal with his speech impediment his entire life, had done his best to help make Tim's surprise induction ceremony a success, and he rewarded Martin by laughing at him. Tim shakes hands with Boo and Louie before he leaves, explaining he has homework. Neither Boo nor Louie says anything, but Tim could see they are disappointed with him.

When Tim arrives home, Veronica is busy in the kitchen.

"You're back early. How did your surprise induction go?" she asks.

"Not very well, Mom," Tim says and goes onto explain what had happened.

"You know I get angry at guys like Tito and Marco for taking advantage of defenseless people, but I guess I am capable of being callously heartless at times."

"Don't be so hard on yourself. You didn't go there with intentions of humiliating Martin, and the fact that the incident is bothering you now says more about you than what happened." "Thanks, Mom. You always know how to put things in a better light," Tim responds as he heads up to his room to begin his studies.

Chapter 17

Infatuation

For the next three weeks, Joan and Tim become nearly inseparable. He waits for her every morning at his hall monitoring location, and she makes sure she is there at the same time every morning. Their conversation is casual. It is more important that they get a chance to see one another before the day of classes start. They usually pass each other in the halls in between classes. They seldom speak but often touch as they pass. His hand reaches out to her hand, or she presses her shoulder against his shoulder.

A month ago, he could not imagine that such a small gesture would have any impact on him, and now, he is walking on air whenever she comes near him. On weekends, he has access to Boo's car. He takes her to school dances, where they both seem to enter into a trance when they are slow dancing or to the movie theater, where they seldom get a chance to watch the movie. Before he returns her home, they spend hours talking or making out. When they return to her house, they both have a difficult time separating.

When he arrives home after a long Saturday night with Joan, Veronica is in the kitchen and is enjoying a cup of tea.

"Mom, what was it like when you met Boo?"

"He simply swept me off my feet. I fell in love with him the first time I went out with him. I was twenty-one years old, and despite all our difficulties, I have never regretted it."

"How did he act toward you?"

"He was a perfect gentleman. He opened doors for me and was very attentive to me. He loved to party, and we would go to parties or dances at least once a week. He was very outgoing. I loved being with him since I was shy when I was young."

"Did he only date you at the time?"

"Yes. Once he started dating me, he didn't go out with anyone else. He first met me at a dance and claims he told a friend when he first saw me that he was going over to ask me to dance, and if I said yes, he would probably marry me some day."

"Do you think that's true?"

"No, but I love hearing it, even now."

"I'm only eighteen. I'm too young to be in love," he responds.

"Love has many forms, Tim. Most first loves don't last long. It tends to be more infatuation than love, and most teenagers move on when the infatuation subsides. Enjoy every minute while it lasts. It could be over in a month or last a lifetime. In either case, you will probably remember it for a lifetime."

"I've gone out with my fair share of girls, but I never have had these feelings before. I hope it lasts longer than a month. I really enjoy being with her," Tim responds.

"You seem to be your better self tonight. How did your day go?" Tim asks.

"It was a yellow day today. My doctor gave me new pills for my depression. He claims they will reduce the amount of downtime. So far, he appears to be right."

Chapter 18

The Acquisition

The following Sunday morning, Tim is up early. When he gets down the stairs, Veronica is already up, and she has made breakfast for him.

"I'm going to 8:30 Mass. Would you like to join me?" Veronica asks.

"I'm going to 12:00 p.m. Mass today. I have other plans this morning," responds Tim. "Mom, now that you are feeling better, I want you to know I'm thinking of buying a used car. I've got a few hundred bucks saved, and I've been looking through the papers for used-car sales." "Did you ask your father about this, Tim?" "Mom, how could he possibly help? I've done a thorough search. Don't worry. I can handle this by myself. I don't want to be dependent on Boo for a car when I'm going out on weekends. More importantly, I want to be able to pick up Joan in the mornings on the way to school. I've contacted a guy from Elmsford who has a 1949 Ford for sale. He is going to drive the car over here this morning, so I can take a look at it."

Veronica leaves for church. Within a few minutes, a 1949 Ford pulls up in front of the house. The motor sounds good to Tim, but the car has a gray coat of primer paint and needs a good paint job. Tim goes outside and introduces himself to the owner. He is about twenty-five years old, and his name is Peter. "This car is a real cherry," Peter explains. "It needs a paint job, but take a close look at the interior." Tim looks inside the car. The interior is immaculate. It looks brand-new.

"Wow, that is impressive," Tim responds.

"I'll tell you what. You get your money in case you're interested in buying, and I'll let you drive the car around, so you can make up your mind to what you want to do," responds Peter.

As they drive around the village, Tim asks, "How is the engine?"

"It's a cherry, just like the interior." Tim presses down on the gas pedal, and the car speeds up.

"It's got good pickup. That's for sure," Tim explains.

"All this car needs is a paint job," responds Peter. "I'll tell you what. I'm asking $350 for this car. I'll give it to you for $250 since it needs a paint job, but you have to make your mind up now. I have other people asking to see it."

"Make it $200, and I'll buy it."

"You drive a hard bargain. How about $225? We can drive to my house, and I'll get the title paper as long as you got the money."

"You got a deal," Tim replies.

Tim drives to Peter's house where Peter locates and signs over the title to the car. Tim hands Peter the $225, and drives away with the title in his hand. When Tim arrives home, Boo is sitting on the front porch.

"Hey, Dad, do you like my new car," Tim yells out as he exits the car.

"It doesn't look that new to me," Boo responds. "Where did you get it?"

"I bought it from a guy in Elmsford."

"Did you have it checked out before you bought it?"

"I drove it around if that's what you mean. It drives nicely, and it has good pickup."

"Son, just to play it safe, I'll call a mechanic friend of mine to check the car out."

"Dad, I already paid for it."

"Don't let that bother you. If there is a problem with the car, we can resolve it with the owner."

Tim doesn't say anything further. He knows it would be a waste of time to confront his father. Boo goes inside, makes a phone call, and within ten minutes, a mechanic pulls up in front of the house.

"Tim, this is Ralf. Ralf, this is my son Tim. Ralf is a mechanic at the Ford dealership in the village. He will give you a complete rundown on this car."

Ralf spends close to a half hour going over the car before giving Tim the bad news.

"Tim, this car is one step away from retiring to a junkyard. It is burning a lot of oil, indicating engine problems. The brakes need replacing. The radiator is leaking. The oil pan needs replacing, the shock absorbers need replacing, and a whole list of other things I won't bother to mention. I'm sorry to have to tell you, but it's better to hear now than find out later."

Boo thanks Ralf and reaches for his wallet. "That's on me, Bob. I owe you for your previous handiwork at my house," Ralf exclaims. After Ralf leaves, another car pulls in front of the house, but the driver does not get out of the car.

"Tim, do you think you can find your way back to this guy's house"

"Yeah, sure Dad."

"Then get in your car and drive back. I'll be right behind you."

Boo goes over to the car that just pulled up, and he gets in the passenger side. When Tim pulls away from the curb, the stranger and Boo begin to follow him. Twenty minutes later, Tim pulls up in front of Peter's house. Boo and the stranger pull up behind him. Boo gets out of the car and tells Tim to remain in his car. Then he knocks on the front door of Peter's house. A minute later, a man opens the door.

"Can I help you?" he asks.

"Mr. Gilchrest, is your son at home?"

"No, he isn't," the man replies.

"My name is Bob Ferrari and my son, earlier today, bought this car from your son. Your son assured my son that the car is in good working order. A mechanic just looked at it, and he says it has many problems. Here is the list of problems. We are returning the car, and I want my son's $225 back."

"Well, Mr. Ferrari, where I come from a deal is a deal."

"Well, Mr. Gilchrest, in the village we come from we don't take advantage of our youngsters, and we don't let anyone else take advantage of them either."

"I suggest you go away before I call the police, Mr. Ferrari."

"I will go away if you want, but if I leave this porch, my friend over there is going to come to collect. Now, who do you want to pay, me or him?"

Boo points over to the direction of the cars. The stranger is now standing along side Tim's cherry car, and he appears to be inspecting the windshield wiper. He is easily six feet five inches tall, is as wide as a truck, and his hand looks as long as the windshield wiper.

Mr. Gilchrest looks out at the stranger, before looking back at the telephone in the hallway, and then back at Boo. He slowly reaches into his pocket and pulls out $225 from his wallet. Boo hands him the title, and tells Tim to leave the keys to the used car and to get in the backseat of the stranger's car. The stranger and Boo jump into the stranger's car, and they head back to Dobbs Ferry. Tim sits in the backseat of the car in disbelief. *Boo uses a strong-arm vicious thug when he wants something?* He asks himself. Tim can't believe it. Boo looks over at the monster driving, and he begins to laugh, and then the stranger begins laughing.

"Bob, you are a piece of work," the stranger manages to get out in between attacks of laughing. "You set the hook in deep this time!" "Yeah, and he went for it hook, line, and sinker," Boo replies, "Son, this is Brian Brady." "Nice to meet you, Brian," Tim replies in a somewhat timid voice. "It's a pleasure meeting a son of Bob Ferrari," Brian responds. "Tim, Brian belongs to our local carpenter's union. He has been foreman on many jobs going as far back as when we worked on the Tappan Zee Bridge. What's the biggest crime that you committed over the years we've known one another, Brian?" "I got two speeding tickets about three years back."

The two men began to laugh again. This time, Tim joins them.

"Here is some advice for you, Son. If you find yourself in a potential conflict, strike quickly and unexpectedly. Bring force or the appearance of force when necessary. You know I don't get into your business much, Son. Let me just say this for the future. If you're about to buy something that is going to cost you a lot of money, go slowly and always bring in the advice of someone who is an expert on the product before you buy. Here is your $225."

"Thanks, Boo. I really appreciate everything you have done today. I think I'll hold back from buying a car for now."

When Tim returns home, Veronica has returned from Mass and is preparing a Sunday lunch of pork chops, sauerkraut, and mashed potatoes in addition to a freshly baked apple pie for dessert. Boo does not return to the house. Instead, he stays in the car with Brian, and they drive off.

"How did your car search go, Tim?" Veronica asks when Tim enters the house.

"Mom, you won't believe what has happened. I already bought a car and drove it home."

"Where is it, Tim?"

"Well, Boo had some guy come over here to inspect it, and it turns out to be a piece of junk. Now, here's the best part. Boo follows me back to the guy's house, and he persuades the guy's father to give me my money back. He hasn't come to my aid like this before. Hell, in four years of footfall, he has never gone to a single game. I still can't believe it."

"Maybe he has more interest in you than you think. He just doesn't know how to show it. Who was that man in the car with you, Tim?"

"One of his carpenter friends, Brian Brady,"

"Looks like we'll be eating lunch alone. He is one of Boo's old drinking buddies," Veronica responds.

"I'll call a few of the guys to join us if you want?" Tim suggests.

"That sounds like a good idea. No need to let all this good food to go waste."

Tim makes a few phone calls, and within twenty minutes, Veronica's lunch guests include Starkey, Bill Moretti, Fred Ferry, and Mike Campi.

"Hey, Tim, I hear you bought a cherry of a car today," Bill comments when everyone sits down to eat. Everyone laughs.

"The word gets out fast around here. It was such a good deal I sold the car within hours for a profit," Tim responds.

"Is anyone, besides Tim old enough to vote?" asks Veronica in an attempt to change the subject.

"No, I'm the only one here who is eighteen," responds Tim.

"I see you have a vote for John Kennedy pin on your blouse. You wouldn't be voting for him because he is Irish and Catholic, now, would you, Mrs. Ferrari?" Mike asks with an Irish accent.

"I'm voting for him because he is a Democrat, and he supports the less fortunate and the unions. The fact that he is a strong family man and is so damn good looking has little to do with it," replies Veronica with a smile.

"Did you see the news? Now, the French have the Atomic bomb. With this Cold War still heating up, we need someone who will stand up to the Russians. My bet is on Nixon when it comes to dealing with the Russian threat to the United States. Did you see Nikita Krushev, pounding his shoe on the table at the United Nations? He was protesting the UN discussions of the Soviet Union's policies toward Eastern Europe. Someone should have shoved his shoe down his big mouth."

"Can anyone say this fast three times?" asks Bill. "If seventy-seven Soviet sonar ships sent seventy-seven missiles skyward, could the seventy-seven missiles reach the US in less than sixty-six seconds?"

"Kennedy has been talking about an American Peace Corps that will go out to the third world countries and help promote peace. That sounds like a great idea, but that's not the guy you want standing in the White House when nutcase Nikita comes calling. Nixon is capable of putting Nikita in a straight jacket and sending him home if he gets out of hand." Tim adds.

"What is Boo, the staunch Democrat, going to say when he finds out his youngest son is a Republican?" Mike asks.

"I'm not a Republican. I'm an Independent," Tim replies.

"What does an Independent say when asked, 'Do you have trouble making up your mind?" Bill asks.

"A sometimes yes and sometimes no," Mike answers in a dumb-sounding voice.

"You guys are just ticked because you can't vote yet," Tim replies.

"The Huntley Brinkley Report said Nixon and Kennedy are going to have a debate on TV in November," responds Bill.

"They also said that the Howdy Doody show is ending. What will be next, the Mickey Mouse Club or even American Bandstand? What is happening to this world?" Starkey asks with a concerned look.

"Hey, not to change the subject, but did you hear Clark Gable died?" Bill asks.

"Yeah, he wasn't that old, was he?" Fred asks.

"I think he was in his early fifties," Tim responds.

"Speaking of things related to the movies, did anyone see 'Psycho' yet. I saw it the other night, and it scared the hell out of me. There is one scene where half the audience jumped out of their seats. I can't tell you anymore than that. You've got to go see it," Starkey comments.

"You think it will win an Academy Award?" Fred asks.

"I don't know. If they have a movie award for movies that make your hair on your neck stand up, it will win," responds Starkey.

"You think it's based on a real story?" Tim asks.

"Who knows, but if it is, there is at least one scary dude out there that I wouldn't want to meet in a dark alley," responds Starkey.

"At least we don't have to worry about anyone like that in our town," Tim replies.

"How would you know if there is?" Starkey asks.

"I guess I wouldn't know. What a depressing thought!" replies Tim.

Chapter 19

The Second Conquest

Monday morning is a beautiful fall day. It is the start of a new week, and the village is bustling with the sights and sounds of everyday life. The Italian bakery shop is open for business, and the smell of fresh baked bread extends halfway up Main Street. Its coffee shops, drugstore counters, and the village diner await the many adults and students that begin their day with a quickly made breakfast and coffee. The students converge on the school from many directions. The aqueduct in the fall, with all its colorful trees, is one of the more breathtaking accesses to the school.

On this morning, in the midst of all the color, Tito waits for his next victim. He remains behind the maple tree until most of the female students have passed by him, savoring each moment and getting more excited when each group of girls pass closely by him totally unaware of his presence. By 8:30 a.m., the beginning of school classes, the flow of potential victims has stopped. Tito continues to wait knowing there is a good chance someone will be late.

Joan Simpson woke up late this morning, and she is running late for school by the time she dresses and finishes her breakfast. To make up for lost time, she decides to take a shortcut to school by going down the hill directly to Main Street. She can cut down the travel time to school by going the route of the aqueduct, where Tito's luck is about to change.

Tito smiles when he sees the now familiar face. *What are the chances she would come this direction,* he thinks as she gets closer and closer. Finally, she is little more than ten feet away. He quickly grabs her from behind and drags her back toward the woods.

He forces her to the ground, warns her not to turn around, and to be quiet. He has plans for what he is going to do to her, but first, he tells her to get up on her knees so he can get at her panties. She struggles to her knees, and he rips off her underwear, and then takes off his pants.

"Please don't hurt me," Joan pleads as he reaches down between her legs. He begins to mount her from behind as he tells her, "Relax and enjoy it, we are going to have a long morning together."

Suddenly, a loud female voice from across the aqueduct shouts out, "Let her go! We can see you, and we have sent for the police." Tito jumps back quickly, pulls his pants back on, and disappears into the woods.

Joan struggles to her feet and runs in the direction of the voice, but there is no one there to meet her. She turns toward the direction of the school and does not stop running until she reaches the girl's locker room, where she keeps spare underwear in her locker. She showers and heads to class. When she reaches the third floor, she sees Tim in the hallway. Until now, not certain what to do, she has acted as if nothing has happened.

When she reaches Tim's side, she can no longer contain herself, and she breaks down crying, while attempting to explain to Tim everything that happened to her. Tim immediately takes her outside to the side of the school, where they can have some privacy. Joan, in between sobs and crying, tells Tim everything that has just occurred. She is thankful that she has been saved from being raped by an unknown Good Samaritan, but she is still further frightened by not knowing who attacked her.

"You can't possibly go to school today. I'll walk you home, but first, we should stop by the police station and report to them everything that has happened. It is important to see them when everything is still fresh in your mind," Tim explains.

"I just want to go home," Joan responds.

"I know you do, but the sooner the police get to this guy, the less likely he will attack you or someone else. Besides, your Good Samaritan has probably already reported it, and they could be looking for you as we speak. I will be right there with you for support."

Tim's words strike home, and Joan summons up enough courage to visit the police station. When the two students enter the police station, they tell the desk sergeant they want to report an attempted rape and want to know if anyone else has reported the incident. The desk sergeant with a blank stare tells them no one has reported an attempted rape and immediately directs them to Detective Daniel O'Neil.

When Detective O'Neil learns the victim is Joan, he requests Tim to return to the waiting room, and then he closes the door in his office, leaving him and Joan alone.

Detective O'Neil is a tall man with a good build and is always meticulously kept. His curly red hair is never out of place, and his clothes are always well pressed. He has a large frame and an Irish face. His attention to details and good memory helps make him an exceptional detective. He can be forceful and demanding during an interview, or he can be sensitive and caring depending on the circumstances.

"Now, I know this has been a frightening and unbearable experience, but I want you to tell me everything that has happened this morning. Leave nothing out. No matter how insignificant it might seem," Detective O'Neil explains.

"Before I begin, I must tell you I didn't even see his face. I have no way of describing to you what he looks like," responds Joan.

"That will make my job more difficult, but it makes you less of a threat to him if he realizes you cannot identify him," replies Detective O'Neil.

Once again, Joan collects herself, and she goes through everything that happened from being late for school, deciding to take a shortcut and to her meeting Tim in the school hallway. When she finishes, Detective O'Neil begins to ask questions.

"Do you think you could recognize his voice if you heard it again?"

"I am not sure."

"Did the Good Samaritan's voice sound familiar?"

"No."

"You said her voice was very loud. How loud was it?"

"It sounded almost like she was speaking into a microphone."

"Could it have been a police bullhorn?"

"No, it wasn't that loud."

While Detective O'Neil continues with his list of questions, Tim sits patiently in the police station waiting area. Until now, his thoughts had been on Joan's safety and mental state. *Who could have done this? Nothing like this happens in our village,* he thinks while his concern for Joan is slowly growing into anger, and his anger is leading to thoughts of vengeance when he finds out who has attacked her.

Having completed his questions, Detective O'Neil realizes Joan's underwear may still be at the site of the attempted rape. He asks her to show him the exact location that the crime occurred. Tim explains that he will be staying with Joan until her parents return home, and Detective O'Neil allows him to come along.

As Joan approaches the site, she grows fearful and backs up pointing to where Tito had jumped her from behind and dragged her backward into the woods. Her underwear is not at the crime site. Tito had doubled back and retrieved it when he realized Joan had not taken it with her when she escaped his grasp.

Detective O'Neil has little to help him at this point. He tells Joan he will keep an eye on the site for the next month to see if any potential suspects turn up in the area. He will also question any potential suspects that are known to spend time in the area. He offers to drive the students back to Joan's house. On the ride to her home, Detective O'Neil asks Tim, "Where were you when all this happened?" Tim replies, "I'm a hall monitor at school, and I was at my monitoring location on the third floor of the high school."

When Joan's mother returns home from shopping, Tim quickly leaves, giving Joan the privacy and time to decide when and how she will tell her mother and father of the horrific attack. While she has much to be fearful about, the situation could have left her in far worse circumstances. She knows she came close to being raped, but who knows what the attacker would have done after raping her.

Chapter 20

In Search of Answers

Veronica is making one of Boo's favorite dishes, Rosemary Chicken, for dinner. It is already 4:30 p.m., so Tim decides to head to the Shamrock House on Main Street, one of Boo's favorite hangouts. Tim wants to remind him that Veronica is making his favorite dish, so he will be home on time and not bring Veronica out of her seven straight days of uptime.

When he enters the Shamrock House, he is surprised to find that Boo has already left. He is about to leave when he notices Father John and Blackie are sitting at the end of the bar. He moves down to the end of the bar and joins them.

"Buy my two friends a round, and I'll have a beer when you get a chance," Tim announces to the bartender.

"You'll have to wait until Rick finishes his advice session with Eddy the plumber," Father John explains.

"Rick looks like he is twenty-one years old. The plumber is three times his age. Why would he want advice from such a young man?" Tim asks.

"Because he has wisdom far beyond his age. Blackie and I are here for a little advice of our own. God bless him," Father John replies.

The bartender finishes his counseling session. Then he pours three beers for Tim and his two friends. "My name is Rick, I remember you in high school when you were younger. You were in ninth grade when I was a senior," Rick says to Tim as he reaches out and shakes Tim's hand.

Suddenly, James Baratto, another WWII veteran, interrupts them. "Well, if it isn't the US Army Rangers. The very boys the 101st Airborne saved during D-Day," he slurs out before he stumbles up to Blackie and Father John.

"The only thing the 101st saved was themselves by hiding in the hedgerows after you limp dicks landed a mile inland instead of on the beaches, where the US Army Rangers saved the day on their way to winning WWII," responds Blackie.

"Okay! Okay! This is going to stop right now," Rick yells out. "I have in my hand an agreement you both signed the last time you two almost wrecked this bar. I'm not going to read it because you both know full well what it says."

"As you recall, if the hint of another skirmish occurs, you have agreed to my solution to resolving the conflict. Gentleman, you have both just placed the resolution to your endless feuding in my hands. My recommendation to this problem is simple. I am proposing a footrace from the Shamrock House down Main Street to the bakery. The winner's division of the army will be recognized as the Shamrock House's number one WWII division heroes, and this feud will end at the finish line. If an outbreak occurs like this again, after the contest, you will be permanently barred from the Shamrock House."

Blackie asks, "How is this meatball going to compete? He is so blitzed he can hardly walk."

"I can beat you with my eyes closed and in a drunken stupor. Count me in," responds James.

"Looks like they're already closed," replies Blackie.

"Okay Blackie. Here's the deal. You have to run backward to make up for James's condition," Rick demands.

"I'll accept that challenge," replies Blackie. "Any US Army Ranger can beat a 101st Airborne stumblebum even if he is running backward. That's a fact, Jack!" Blackie adds.

"My name's not Jack. So Jack off, Jack!" quips James.

"Okay, okay, both you guys have agreed to the arrangement," Rick announces.

"Nick, you go up Main Street to block oncoming traffic, and Peter, you go down Main Street to block any oncoming traffic," Rick yells down the bar to the two local regulars.

"Are you crazy? We've got fifteen minutes before the rush-hour train traffic comes up in Main," Peter responds.

"That makes your job all the more important," responds Rick.

"Peter, you will also call the winner at the finish line. Here is some chalk. Draw a line on the street at the beginning of the bakery. Nick, here is some chalk for the starting line. You will also be the starter."

"Now," Rick proclaims, turning back to the US Army Ranger and the 101st Airborne antagonist, "both of you squabbling war heroes get outside on the starting line." Within minutes, the race is set to go. The entire bar empties out, and bets have already been made.

"On your mark, get set, go!" Nick shouts in a very official-sounding tone.

James runs very slowly, stumbling first to the left, then to the right, just enough to somehow remain in the center of the street. On each stumble, the crowd responds with a whooo, while Blackie continues to run backward in a straight line making sure he is always five feet ahead of James. At the halfway mark, Blackie rolls down his shirtsleeve, retrieves a cigarette from his pack of Marlboros, and rolls the cigarette pack back up into his shirtsleeve. He lights the cigarette while remaining five feet ahead of James. "Go, Rangers," Father John shouts from the sidelines.

As they near the finish line, Blackie raises his arms in a sign of victory, and his pack of cigarettes flies out of his shirtsleeve, landing behind him. On his next backward step, his right heel lands on the pack of cigarettes, and his feet come out from underneath him. He falls on his back, and the back of his head hits the ground. He is momentarily knocked unconscious. After a few seconds, he struggles to his feet just in time to see James stumble over the finish line.

Peter holds up James's hand and proclaims the 101st Airborne to be the Shamrock House's number one WWII army division heroes; then he holds up Blackie's arm, and he declares the US Army Rangers to be the Shamrock House's number two army division heroes.

Blackie accepts second place as a onetime exception for having lost in a fair race. James and Blackie laugh, while they walk back to the bar with an arm over each other's shoulder partly as a display of a new friendship and partly for support.

Tim stops Father John before he returns to the bar.

"Can I ask you a private question?" Tim asks. "I need some answers to a troubling problem."

"Of course," Father John replies.

Tim's relationship with his father is strained to the point that he will not seek Boo's advice on personal matters. While Father John has a quirky side, he is capable of giving sound advice.

"How would you handle a situation where someone attacks a girlfriend of yours, and she can't identify the attacker? Would you let the police resolve the problem, or would you attempt, on your own, to find out who it is and serve up your own justice?"

"I would do everything I could to help the police, but I would leave police work to the police."

"Wouldn't you be worried that the attacker might go after her again before the police get around to solving who it is?" Tim asks.

"Tim, this unknown person could be as dangerous to you as he is to her. I would leave it in the hands of the people who are experienced in these matters."

"I'll give your advice some thought. Thank you for your time," Tim replies

"Bless you, my boy," Father John responds as he enters the bar. Tim turns and heads home.

Chapter 21

The Third Conquest

For four weeks, Tim leaves his house early, so he can meet Joan close to her home when she walks to school. They never walk in the direction of the aqueduct, and Tim constantly looks in all directions trying to determine if anyone is following them. There is no sign of them being followed during the four weeks. Tim is beginning to relax on the way to school.

Tito has stayed away from the aqueduct and the high school out of fear the police might be waiting for him. The police, on the other hand, have no idea who the suspect is. However, Detective O'Neil, along with two of the village police officers take turns during the day to stake out the site of the attempted rape in an effort to identify a suspect or even catch him in the act. After four weeks, they decide to drop the surveillance and get busy interviewing potential suspects.

At the end of a month of lying low, Tito is getting restless. He has modified his plans for his next attack. He will not spend any time near the edge of the woods after he retrieves his next victim to help avoid being seen. The police have not questioned him, and he has not heard of any talk of an attempted rape. *She is probably too afraid to tell the police. She can't even tell them what I look like,* he muses as he dresses. Tito is certain whoever witnessed his last attempted rape must have been too far away to identify him and has not called the police.

It is Thursday morning. Tito finishes dressing, and for the first time in a month, he returns to his favorite spot on the aqueduct. Fortunately for him, the police have stopped surveillance three days ago.

He arrives late and doesn't have to wait long. Anna Rossi, a high school senior, has spent too much time at breakfast and is running late. Anna is an intelligent girl who is at the top of her class academically and has just received a scholarship to college. Her serious attitude about schoolwork is hidden in her warm and friendly personality. She seems to spread joy wherever she goes, and everyone in the village likes her.

Tito hands are beginning to sweat, while he waits for her to come closer. As she passes the maple tree, Tito reaches out, lifts her up from behind, and pulls her into the woods. He slams her down onto the ground, warns her to close her eyes, and not to look back, or he will hurt her. She obeys. He blindfolds her, lifts her up from behind, again, and takes her deeper into the woods to a designated location. It is a small clearing in the midst of the woods that he has prepared for her.

After he disappears into the woods, a figure from the opposite side of the aqueduct rises, crosses the aqueduct, and moves in his direction. Rosanne has a butcher knife in her hand instead of a megaphone, and she plans on stopping him before he rapes again. When she reaches the area where Tito had raped her, she realizes he is not there.

A chill runs down her spine, but it does not stop her from moving forward. He has taken Anna into the woods. Where has he gone, and how can she find him? There are no screams coming from the woods to help direct her, so she decides to move slowly in one direction, then double back if she can't find them and try another direction. Twenty-five minutes later, after doubling back twice and heading in a third direction, she sees a blue shoe just before a small opening in the woods. She picks up the shoe and moves slowly, gripping her knife tightly. As she enters the clearing, it is unnervingly quiet as if all the other creatures in the woods know something is wrong.

Halfway through the clearing, she slightly stumbles. Her ankle has twisted on a firm object beneath her foot. She looks down and the hair on her neck rises. The object is Anna's leg. Anna has been covered with leaves. Rosanne uncovers her head. She is lying face up, and she is dead.

Rosanne's anger turns to terror. At first, she cannot move. *Where is Tito? Is he watching me or waiting for me to move? Am I going to be the next victim?* Her mind is racing. She must get out of the woods. She turns and runs toward the aqueduct as fast as her frightened feet will carry her. When she reaches the aqueduct, she drops Anna's shoe where someone will almost certainly find it. Hopefully, the shoe will lead a search party in the direction of Anna's body.

She continues running until she reaches the safety of the schoolyard. *There is a good chance Tito left the area before I arrived,* she reasons. *He does not suspect I know he raped me. If I tell the police what has happened, he will kill me next. I must have time to think.*

Chapter 22

My Daughter is Missing

By 4:30 p.m., Anna has not returned home, and her mother, Marie Rossi, is worried. Anna is seldom late. She arrives home almost everyday at 3:45 p.m. On occasion, if she is going to be late, she lets her mother know before she leaves for school in the morning, or she calls from school if something unexpected comes up.

Mrs. Rossi calls the school at 4:45 p.m., only to learn from the administration office that Anna had not reported to school today. Stricken with panic, she immediately calls the police.

"Help me! My daughter is missing," she explains to the desk sergeant that answers the phone.

"How long has she been missing?" the sergeant asks.

"Since this morning. She did not report to school today."

"I suggest you call around to her friends. In most cases, the child has visited a friend without letting a parent know."

"My daughter never goes anywhere without contacting me first," explains Marie. "You must help me!"

"Ma'am, our procedures require that we don't do anything until at least forty-eight hours have passed. She probably will show up tonight. Give us a call on Saturday morning if she still isn't home."

Marie hangs up, but she isn't about to wait around. She decides to retrace her daughter's daily walk to school. She walks up Main Street, stopping at shops along the way, and asking if anyone has seen Anna. Two of the shopkeepers say they had seen her in the morning, and both remembered that she was late for school.

At the top of Main Street, Marie Rossi enters the path to the aqueduct. The Gallente brothers, Frank and Chuck, are returning home from the high school and are walking toward Marie. They enjoy a little game each day when they reach the aqueduct. One brother throws an object found on the aqueduct in the air and the other throws rocks at it. Frank bends over and picks up Anna Rossi's blue shoe. He tosses it up in the air in the direction of the woods, and Chuck manages to throw three rocks at it. The last rock hits the target, and the shoe falls short of the woods. Marie Rossi walks by the Gallente brothers seconds later.

When Marie reaches the school, she finds all the offices are closed. She will have to return tomorrow for more information on Anna's school activities and to question some of her friends to determine what has happened to Anna.

Marie Rossi, like her daughter, is an intelligent woman who realizes she will have to put her emotions aside and use every bit of her intelligence to uncover what has happened to her daughter. Marie is small in stature and has a very light voice, but her communication skills and direct approach with people make her a commanding force that she calls upon when needed.

Chapter 23

A Word to the Wise

On the night of Anna's disappearance, Tim is sitting quietly at home when the phone rings. When Tim answers the phone, a muffled voice of a young girl begins the conversation.

"Listen to me and listen very carefully. Do not interrupt. Do not say anything until I am done talking. The same person that has attacked your girlfriend has attacked me and now, Anna Rossi. Only this time, he has murdered Anna. Joan and I are in danger of him killing us if he suspects we can identify him. He is so demented and devious he may kill us even if he thinks we can't identify him. We simply represent loose ends to him."

"Who is this?"

"Shut up! I told you not to speak until I'm done! It's not important who I am. What is important is that you know who the killer is and that you act before he does. The sick pervert is Tito Menetti. He is good at covering his tracks. If we report him to the police, it will take time for the police to find enough evidence to arrest him. In the meantime, your girlfriend's life and my life will be at risk, while this nut is still loose.

"He is good at eluding the police too. For the last month, the police have staked out the spot on the aqueduct where he hangs out, and he never showed up when they were there. A few days after the police dropped their surveillance he returned to his hideout. When he does show up, he appears to be certain his hiding spot is safe. He has even fallen asleep there one time.

"He must have a means of knowing what the police are doing. His belief that he is secure at his aqueduct hideout makes him vulnerable to attack at that very same place. Why don't you give some thought tonight to whether you want to help me go after him before he strikes out at Joan!

"I will call you back tomorrow morning for your decision, and depending on your decision, I will let you know who I am. The police do not know yet that Anna has been murdered. A word to the wise, don't tell anyone of this phone call.

"You must be concerned about Joan's safety by now. He is an animal. He grabbed me from behind and ripped off my underwear the same way he did to Joan. Only I wasn't as lucky as Joan. If he decides to go after her again, I'm sure he will rape her before he kills her."

Before Tim can ask a question, he hears a click. Tim immediately calls information and gets Anna's phone number and dials it.

"Hello, Mrs. Rossi, is Anna home?" Tim asks when Mrs. Rossi answers the phone.

"Who is this," Mrs. Rossi asks.

"It's Tim Ferrari. I'm just calling to give Anna our chemistry homework assignment since she wasn't in class today."

"Tim, she went to school today, but she hasn't returned home yet. Would you have any idea where she is?"

"No," Tim responds.

"What time is chemistry class?" Mrs. Rossi asks.

"It begins at 2:30."

"Can you recall seeing her anytime earlier during the day?"

"No, I can't say I have."

"Tim, if any of your friends can recall seeing her during the day, please call me. I must go now. I am waiting for many return calls."

The phone clicks, and Tim's hand is frozen to the phone when he realizes Joan's life might be in serious danger.

Chapter 24

The Executioner Awaits

The following morning, Tito is up early and out of the house by 7:00 a.m. He knows the police will be combing the woods in an attempt to locate Anna, and he finds great excitement in returning to his hideout one more time before they arrive in the area.

On his way up lower Main Street, he is surprised to find Marco is also up early.

"Tito, can I ask you a favor?"

"What is it, Marco?"

"Can I borrow your pellet gun?"

"What for?" Tito asks.

"I want to use it, along with my trusted blade to finish off Tim's dog. It's been living in the woods for the past few months."

"Here, only don't kill it. Bring the dog to me, and we'll finish it off my way."

"Are you going to your hangout at the maple tree?" Marco asks.

Tito lunges at Marco, knocking him to the ground. He puts his hands around Marco's neck, and begins to squeeze.

"How do you know where I spend my private time?" Tito growls as he continues to choke Marco.

"I followed you the other day."

"Don't you ever mention my hideout again, and if you ever tell anyone I was there, I will kill you. Do you hear me?"

"Yes! Yes! I hear you. Let me go, I can't breathe!"

Tito releases Marco and shouts, "Get out of my sight before I do something to you now."

Marco leaves without telling Tito he had nailed two wooden boards to the maple tree, so Tito can remain hidden and have a better view of the aqueduct from the branches of the tree.

Tito walks up Main Street, and then down to his favorite spot on the aqueduct. It's a short distance from home. It is only 7:20 a.m., much too early to watch for students on their way to class. He leans against the maple tree that so often helps hide him from view. He is unaware of the two wooden boards that Marco has nailed to the opposite side of the tree and has decided he will have to find a new site for future conquests. He had stayed up late going over and over what he had done, while fondling a personal object he has taken from his victim. Without a full night's sleep, in a few minutes he is half asleep. His head drops, causing him to wake and lean against the maple tree. He opens his eyes wide and shakes his head to be certain he is awake.

Soon his eyes begin to close again. As his head leans forward, a yellow belt slowly descends from the branches of the maple tree. The end of the belt has been run through the belt buckle making a noose. The first belt buckle hole has been enlarged. A rope has been threaded through the enlarged belt buckle hole and is held tight by a strong knot. A pair of hands reaches down out of the branches and quickly fits the noose over Tito's head and around his neck. Startled, Tito opens his eyes and begins to reach for the belt. At the same time, the executioner jumps from the tree in between two branches with the other end of the rope tied around his waist, instantly causing the noose to tighten around Tito's neck. Then, the rope jerks up into the tree, lifting Tito a foot off the ground and away from the tree trunk. He tries to loosen the belt by wrapping both hands around it and pulling, but the weight of his body makes the effort useless. The homemade hangman's noose will not break Tito's neck. He will not die quickly. He will slowly die like many of the animals he has tortured. The executioner, having just completed a next to impossible task, waits patiently while Tito dangles from the tree and slowly chokes to death from the weight of his own body.

When the executioner is certain Tito is dead, he cuts the rope and retrieves the belt from around Tito's neck. He lays Tito flat on the ground to avoid any passerby from seeing his body. Then he vanishes into the woods making sure he has left nothing behind. It is a day of reckoning.

From an embankment across the aqueduct, up on a hill, Rosanne has been watching the execution unfold. She arrived at her usual time, 7:30 a.m., at her hidden vantage point and was surprised to see Tito was already at his favorite spot. She expected him to return to the scene of the crime but not this early. She can see that Tito is already comfortable and is leaning against the tree. When he wraps his hands around his neck, she doesn't realize what is happening until his body begin to sway, his feet are not on the ground, and he is being hung by a yellow belt attached to a rope.

You son of a bitch, Ferrari! You son of a bitch! I didn't think you had it in you! she whispers to herself. She decides not to go down to the site until he leaves. He still doesn't know her identity and would rather leave it that way for now. Tito dies slowly, so the wait seems forever. Rosanne begins to worry that the morning school traffic will soon begin on the aqueduct, and someone will notice Tito hanging from the tree. Suddenly his body drops to the ground. The executioner appears briefly, removes the yellow belt from Tito's neck, and disappears into the woods.

Rosanne waits twenty minutes to be certain he has left the area. Then she quickly descends the hill, crosses the aqueduct, and arrives at the maple tree with her knife in her hand. Tito isn't moving. She moves up close to him and whispers. "Look at you now, you disgusting pig. God knows how many lives you have destroyed or ended." In a moment of relief and unending anger, she kneels down and plunges her knife repeatedly into his groin. "You will have to report to a much higher judge now, and may he treat you the same way you treated everyone on earth." She slowly stands up, walks up to the aqueduct, and turns toward the direction of high school.

Chapter 25

It's Time to Act

M arie Rossi and her husband enter the police station at 9:30 a.m. She has already been to the high school, and she has spoken to as many students as she could find that are in Anna's classes. No one had seen her anywhere on the school grounds or in the village yesterday.

She immediately asks for Detective O'Neil. He comes out of his office to meet her. Before he can say anything, she demands that he act on the disappearance of her daughter by beginning to try to locate her.

"My daughter is not the type of girl who would run off. There is nothing missing from her room to indicate she ran away. All she had with her yesterday was her schoolbooks. From calling on her classmates, I have learned there was an attempted rape last month on the aqueduct. If this is true, you must act now. Help me find my daughter!" she demands as her voice begins to rise. "Search the woods! Check throughout the village! Do whatever you have to do, but start now! Don't tell me about your useless rules!" she demands. "My daughter is missing!"

Despite her angry mood and contempt for the police force, Detective O'Neil realizes she is in need of help, and he assures her he will act immediately. He asks Marie for a list of the clothes Anna was wearing yesterday. When she completes the list, it includes a pair of blue shoes. He tells Marie and her husband to go home, and he will call them in the afternoon to update them on his progress. He asks Marie to get to a printing shop before noon and to have a hundred copies of a most recent picture of Anna made with the words, "Missing, call Dobbs Ferry Police," and include the police phone number.

He and his men will begin by searching the woods. He decides to start where the attempted rape had occurred to see if there is any indication of a recent struggle. When he and police officers John Romano and Raymond McEntire approach the maple tree, they move off the aqueduct, keeping their eyes to the ground as they reach within twenty yards of the tree. Officer Romano stops, slowly bends down, and then holds up Anna's blue shoe. Holding it with two fingers, he quickly places the shoe in a plastic evidence bag.

They pick up the pace, partly expecting to find more potential evidence of foul play near the maple tree site. As they converge on the tree, they can see an area that is trampled down. In it is the body of Tito Menetti. Detective O'Neil is taken aback by what he sees while relieved it isn't Anna.

"Tito Menetti, I would have expected him to be a perpetrator, not a victim," he explains, shaking his head in disbelief.

Detective O'Neil asks the officers to remain still; he wants as little disturbance of the murder scene as possible. He slowly walks over to the body, making certain he does not step on any potential evidence. He checks Tito's pulse to see if there is any sign of life. Tito is dead.

"Officer Romano, go back and alert the station. We have a murder on our hands. Make sure Chief Nolan is immediately informed regardless of where he might be. Call the Town of Greenburgh police department and tell them we will need the help of their officers who have crime scene investigation training and experience and bring back a coroner, a camera, and a bloodhound to help us find whoever belongs to this blue shoe. Call the DA and get a search warrant for these woods before you do anything else."

"Officer McEntire, I want you to secure this crime scene. Cordon off the crime scene area, and don't let anyone through except the people who are assigned to this case. Nothing at this scene should be moved or touched unless absolutely necessary, so get whoever has to enter the scene to walk in the same path to the body as I did to avoid contamination of evidence.

Get your notepad out and be ready to take notes. I want you to work with the Greenburgh crime scene experts by taking notes of every piece of potential evidence they find here. You must identify each piece of evidence and the time when it is found. Take a picture of it, and place it in its own evidence bag. I also want you to take notes of everyone who enters the scene; who they are, when they entered, and what is their responsibility at the scene. Before removing the deceased, make sure they examine him for physical evidence, including loose hair, fibers, etc. Take your time. There is no reason to hurry. Also collect his personal effects, wallet, jewelry, etc. Finally, you will be responsible for reporting the results of the investigation to me or to Detective Sergeant Pascutti if he arrives before I return."

Within twenty minutes, Officer Romano returns with the coroner, the camera, and a bloodhound. Two Greenburgh crime scene investigators arrive minutes later. The coroner begins processing the deceased, while the Greenburgh crime scene investigators process the crime scene. Officer McEntire assists the coroner and the Greenburgh crime scene investigators by taking pictures of the body and helping process any evidence found.

When Detective O'Neil is about to begin the search for the owner of the blue shoe, Chief Nolan arrives at the scene. Detective O'Neil quickly updates him on the status of the investigation.

When Chief Nolan is satisfied that Detective O'Neil has control of the crime scene, he adds, "We'll place an officer at the top of Main Street to keep traffic flowing and reduce the amount of onlookers that are going to be drawn to the murder site. We'll also cordon off the entrance to the aqueduct to avoid a mob scene down here. I want you back at my office as soon as you are done down here to update me on your findings. Get over to the Menetti house as soon as time permits to notify the parents on the death of their son. I'll wait here until you return with that bloodhound, and I will answer any questions of the press who will probably be here soon."

The bloodhound is given a good whiff of Anna's blue shoe. It circles the area for a minute or two, and then goes directly into the woods with O'Neil and Romano following. Within five minutes, the dog enters the clearing where the body of Anna lays partly covered with leaves.

"Oh no," Detective O'Neil murmurs as he enters the clearing, "It can't be! It can't be!"

He has been on the Dobbs Ferry police force for twenty years, and during that time, there has not been a single murder. Now, he has uncovered two murders in a single day. Once again, he slowly walks over to the body to be certain she is dead. When he touches her arm, it is stiff. She has been dead for some time. He gives Officer Romano the same set of instructions he had just given Officer McEntire, and then returns to the maple tree crime scene.

He updates Chief Nolan on the discovery of a second murder victim. He tells the coroner and the Greenburgh police they have more work to do at the second murder site, and asks Officer McEntire to review with him and Chief Nolan what his team has uncovered. "It looks like this guy was both hung from the tree and stabbed in the groin with a very sharp knife. The hanging is what in all likelihood killed him. We will be able to give you more info after an autopsy is complete. This site is empty of any evidence. Someone spent time to make sure no finger prints would be found on the body or anywhere else and no shoe prints, or any objects were left on the ground or in the tree. However, there is what appears to be a rope mark on the tree limb where it branches out about five feet from the trunk of the tree, and there are two small pieces of wood nailed to the opposite side of the tree that may have been used to help one of the perpetrators climb the tree. There were no fingerprints on the wood. The two pieces of wood appear to be from the same cut of lumber. The victim has tree bark under his nails, and his personal effects included a pair of gold earrings," Officer McEntire reports.

Chief Nolan and Detective O'Neil commend Officer McEntire on his thoroughness in managing the crime site. "Detective Pascutti should be arriving shortly, and I want you to make him responsible for managing both crime sites, while you notify both the victims' relatives of their deaths before they hear it from someone else." Chief Nolan explains to Detective O'Neil. Then he heads up to the entrance to the aqueduct, where several reporters wait for an update on what has happened.

Minutes later, an ambulance and police car driving south on the aqueduct, having entered from a northern access point near the golf course, stop adjacent to the maple tree. Detective Sgt. Anthony Pascutti exits the police car and meets with Detective O'Neil. Anthony Pascutti is, without question, the most intelligent member of the force. His low-key personality and his easy mannerism disguise his true nature. He is the hunter of truth who is dedicated to solving crime. His passion for his work is exceeded only by his intellect. His strong reasoning and memory skills make him a perfect match for detective work. Detective O'Neil immediately updates Detective Pascutti on the status of the investigation. He asks Detective Pascutti to manage both murder investigations until he returns. "I have to notify the parents of the deceased," he explains.

When Detective O'Neil has left the scene of the murder, Officer McEntire murmurs, "This morning we were Ray and John at breakfast. Now we're Officer McEntire and Officer Romano. This guy takes his job a little too serious at times."

"I know what you mean," replies Detective Pascutti whom Officer McEntire and Officer Romano respect and have reported to for years. "He is carrying a lot of weight on his shoulders, and he may act different under these circumstances. Right now, he needs as much support as we can give him."

"Then maybe someone should explain to him that we have had training in crime scene investigation," replies Officer Romano. "I realize there hasn't been any need to use the training for felony investigation, so I'm going to give him the benefit of the doubt that he is only trying to be helpful."

Chapter 26

A Moment of Silence

Detective O'Neil decides to walk back to the village. Anna's home is on Palisades Street. Palisades Street runs parallel to Main Street. The five-minute walk will give him time to prepare mentally for what he has to do. He has known Anna since she was a little baby. She was a polite and intelligent child and always greeted everyone with a warm smile. He has had to notify parents of the death of their child on numerous other occasions due to car accidents or drowning but never for murder. He dreads mostly that moment of silence that occurs when he utters the word dead. The mind cannot initially grasp or accept the unthinkable enormity of one's child dying. It usually shuts down for a moment. Then in a blink of an eye just about any reaction can occur. In many cases, a parent will scream, or collapse, or just refuse to believe it is true. It is a moment that he does his best to divorce his emotions and remain professional. Today is going to be the most difficult day to maintain his composure. Anna was such a sweet young lady.

After a good brisk walk, he is prepared for the most difficult part of his job. He arrives at Anna's front door and rings the bell. Mrs. Rossi opens the door.

"Mr. O'Neil, come in, I have a sample flyer to show you. Come in."

"Is your husband home?" he asks stepping inside.

"Yes, John, can you come downstairs? Detective O'Neil is here."

As John reaches the downstairs foyer, Detective O'Neil in a very low and calm voice says, "We have found your daughter, and I am here to regretfully inform you she is dead."

For a brief moment, there is complete silence as if the world has stopped.

"Oh no! No! It can't be!" Mrs. Rossi gasps. The flyer slides from her hands and drifts to the floor in what seems like an eternity.

Her husband puts his arms around her to keep her steady.

"How did this happen?" John asks.

"We found her body in the woods, off the aqueduct. She is a murder victim." Detective O'Neil replies.

"Oh dear God! Do you know who did this to her?"

"No, not yet, but we have already begun an investigation."

"This can't be!" Mrs. Rossi repeats, "I want to go see her."

"When her body is transferred to the morgue, you will be called to identify her."

"The morgue. The morgue," Mrs. Rossi repeats before her legs give out, and she collapses in her husband's arms.

John carries his wife to the living room couch, lays her down, and then goes to the kitchen to get her water.

"Mr. O'Neil, if there is anything we can do to help, please call on us. Right now, I must attend to my wife"

"John, if I can have a minute of your time now. It might be helpful. Did anyone make any kind of verbal or even physical threat to her recently?"

"No, Anna has no enemies that we know of."

Detective O'Neil holds up the small plastic bag containing the earrings found in Tito's Jacket. "Do these look familiar to you?"

"Yes, they are Anna's earrings," John gasps.

"I have to keep these earrings for now. I know there is nothing I can say that will properly express my condolences. I can't possibly know what you are experiencing now.

"I want you to know that I and everyone on the police force will do whatever we have to do to solve this crime, find the person responsible for this horrific deed and bring closure for you and your wife."

"Thank you, for your support."

Detective O'Neil closes the door behind him. He had done his best to remain divorced of feelings, but this is a close village, and his last words reflect how overcome he is by Anna's death. There is a good chance Tito is the person responsible for this despicable crime and the attempted rape of Joan Simpson. He must get to Tito's house immediately. Tito may have kept other items of his victims.

Walking at a fast pace, he arrives at Tito's house in less than ten minutes. When he knocks on the door, Tito's mother answers.

"Mrs. Menetti, I am Detective O'Neil from the Dobbs Ferry police station. Is your husband home?" O'Neil asks.

"I know who you are. Is Tito in any kind of trouble? My husband is inside."

"May I come in? I would like to speak to you together."

"Come in," she replies as her husband, Mario, walks into the kitchen.

Detective O'Neil follows Mrs. Menetti into the kitchen. When both husband and wife sit down at the kitchen table, O'Neil remains standing. "I'm afraid I'm not here because Tito is in trouble. This morning, just off the aqueduct, we found Tito. He is dead. He was murdered."

A moment passes, and then Mrs. Menetti begins to scream. It is a scream that only a mother can make for a child. It is a scream full of desperation, denial, grief, and anger. Mario gently places his arms around her, and her screams slowly reduce to sobs.

"Do you know who killed him?" Mario asks.

"No, but we have already begun working on solving this crime," he responds.

"If you would allow me to search his room, I might be able to find some clues to what happened today. If you feel this is an inappropriate time, I will certainly understand."

"If it might help, go ahead. It's upstairs on the left," Mario responds, as he continues to console his wife.

"Do you mind signing this paper indicating you have given me permission to search Tito's room?" he asks handing Mario a pen. Mario signs the paper and turns his attention back to his wife. Mario's permission allows Detective O'Neil to enter Tito's room without requiring a search warrant, and Detective O'Neil wants proof that he gave his permission. Worried that Mario might change his mind; he quickly climbs the stairs and enters Tito's room. He is hoping to find more evidence of Tito's conquests. It doesn't take long to find his evidence. The middle dresser drawer has a bracelet, two pairs of torn panties, and a bra hidden in the back. He takes pictures of the room, the dresser, and the items in the drawer. He places each one of the items in separate evidence bags, and then he places all of the plastic evidence bags in a brown bag. When he is done, he quietly returns to the first floor foyer.

"The coroner's office will call you this afternoon. I know this will be difficult to do, but you will be requested to go to the morgue to identify Tito's body. I have some items here that might shed light on what happened. I am leaving a list of them on the foyer table. I will contact you if we need more information," he explains before he exits the house.

It is difficult for him to have as much empathy for Tito's parents as he has for Anna's parents, knowing Tito has in all probability murdered Anna. Mario has been arrested a number of times over the years, including for beating his wife. However, Detective O'Neil is taken aback by the concern and gentleness Mario displayed for his wife during this immense family tragedy.

Within ten minutes, he arrives back at the first crime scene. He stops at one of the empty squad cars, calls the police station, and tells them to get a search warrant for the home of Tito Menetti as further coverage for the search he did of Tito's room. He wants the search warrant as backup in case Mr. Menetti decides to protest against having his son's room searched. Both crime scenes have been processed, and both bodies have been shipped to the morgue. Detective O'Neil meets with Detective Pascutti and police officers John Romano and Raymond McEntire for a review of each crime scene.

"Here is what we have so far," explains Detective Pascutti. "As you already know, the Tito site has turned up little in terms of evidence. Tito was strangled to death by being hung from a branch on the maple tree. From the marks on his neck, it looks like a belt was placed around his neck, and somehow a rope was attached to the belt and hung over the branch of the tree. He must have died a very slow death, since his neck was not snapped in this very crude method of hanging him. He was cut down from the tree. The belt was removed, and sometime later, he was stabbed three times in the groin. We are certain the coroner's report will verify our finding that he first died from hanging then was stabbed, and he should be able to tell us just how long after Tito was dead that he was stabbed. In any case, the knife wounds could not have caused his death."

"So, either the individual or individuals who hung him cleared the area of evidence, then stabbed him, or the individual who stabbed him came along after the hanging," Detective O'Neil theorizes.

"Whether one or multiple people committed this felony, it appears to be an act of vengeance," responds Detective Pascutti. "It's not likely a single person murdered him. A single person could have knocked Tito out, put the belt around his neck, and then hung him. However, there are no contusions or bruises to his body other than the marks around his neck. He had to be conscious when he was hung. The bark under his fingernails indicate he attempted to hold onto the tree, and the nail marks around the belt line marks on his neck indicate he tried to pull the belt loose. Someone must have kept him at gunpoint, while another perpetrator hung him."

"If that's the case, why didn't they tie his arms behind his back? It would have made their job a lot easier. Why didn't they just throw the rope up over the tree limb instead of climbing the tree?" asks Detective O'Neil.

"Maybe the hangman wasn't very strong and jumped from the tree, while holding onto the rope as a means of hanging him," responds Detective Pascutti. "Maybe the hangman was a woman."

"A single person with a gun could have waited in the tree until Tito arrived at the scene, and then have forced Tito to put the belt around his neck before the perpetrator jumped off the limb," replies O'Neil.

"Yes, that's possible but less plausible," responds Detective Pascutti.

"Where do we stand on Anna's site?" Detective O'Neil asks.

"The second site is more promising," responds Detective Pascutti. "We have found finger prints and sneaker prints in the crime scene area. The sneaker prints are an exact match to the sneakers Tito is wearing, and the fingerprints on a dead tree branch match Tito's fingerprints. The girl was raped and strangled to death. The coroner has determined the perpetrator's blood type from his semen, and it matches Tito's blood type. Her bra and panties were not on her or in the crime scene area."

"We can add to the report that the earrings found on Tito's body belong to Anna," adds Detective O'Neil. "I have also located a bra, two pairs of torn panties, and a bracelet in Tito's bedroom. I'm sure we will find the bra and one pair of panties belong to Anna. Let's get the investigation report together on this one as quick as possible. There is overwhelming evidence that Tito committed this crime. The sooner we get all our findings together, the sooner we can make our report to the DA. We have a lot on our plate right now, and since this one points so clearly to Tito, let's get it closed so we can focus on who killed Tito," Detective O'Neil explains with a sense of relief.

"John and Ray, as investigating officers of your assigned sites, can you put together the evidence section of your respective reports, and Anthony, can you write the summary for each investigation site? I will tie up the remaining loose ends of the evidence I located at Tito's bedroom. Let's try to get Anna's report to the DA by Sunday morning," Detective O'Neil requests.

All three men agree they will do their best to meet the deadline.

"Check for fingerprints on these items from Tito's dresser before we leave," Detective O'Neil asks the Greenburgh investigating officers. Within ten minutes, the investigating officers return with the results. Tito's fingerprints are located on the bracelet and on one of the panties. Before going home and calling it a day, he decides to return to Anna's house with the articles located in Tito's dresser drawer. Her mother is able to identify the bra and one pair of panties as belonging to Anna.

He takes the remaining pair of underwear and the bracelet to Joan Simpson's home, and she identifies the underwear as hers. It is the one with Tito's fingerprints on it. *The bracelet must belong to another victim that has not come forward or is dead,* he assumes.

By the time he returns to the police station, the coroner's office has reported its findings. Tito died from being hung from the tree, and then approximately one hour later was stabbed in the groin. Detective O'Neil updates Chief Nolan on the status of the investigation, and then returns home for some needed rest.

Chapter 27

The Day After

On Saturday morning, Tim rises early to get mentally ready for the day's football game against Edgemont High School. They are normally an easy team to beat, but this year they have built a reputation for being an aggressive team. When Tim is about to make breakfast, the phone rings. He quickly answers the phone, thinking the caller is probably the girl that contacted him Thursday night. The caller is Starkey.

Before Tim can say hello, Starkey asks him, "Have you read the paper yet?"

"No, I haven't," Tim replies.

"The police found two people murdered off the aqueduct behind the school yesterday—Tito Menetti and Anna Rossi. Someone hung Tito from a tree, and then stabbed him in the groin for good measure. The DA has just about closed the case on Anna's murder. They have extensive evidence that Anna was killed the day before yesterday by Tito, and they believe Tito was killed yesterday by someone who was looking for revenge, possibly for Anna's murder or for a previous crime Tito committed. They also have evidence that it was Tito who attacked Joan. Tim, the police will be calling on you, since you have been dating Joan. Make sure you have a good alibi for where you were early yesterday morning. Tito was murdered around 7:30 yesterday morning."

"That's no problem. I can't believe that wacko killed Anna. He must have attacked her from behind like he did to Joan, and then dragged her into the woods. Joan was lucky she had a Good Samaritan that day."

"I wonder who is the Good Samaritan?" Starkey asks.

"Maybe the Good Samaritan killed Tito," Tim adds, "This is insane, isn't it?"

"Do you know if the game is called off?" Tim asks.

"Anna's parents told the principal to go ahead with all school activities. They feel that Anna would want all activities to continue. There will be a viewing tonight and tomorrow. She will be buried on Monday morning. The high school will be closed all day Monday," Starkey replies.

"Thanks for the call, Starkey."

"See you later," Starkey replies and hangs up the phone.

Tim sits quietly next to the phone for sometime before it rings again.

"Hello," he says still in private thought.

"It looks like Joan will be safe now, and so will I," Rosanne says with a display of joy in her voice.

Tim sits up in his chair.

"You got your wish. Didn't you!" Tim replies.

"Yes, I did! Yes, I did! He deserves everything he got."

"Where and when would you like to meet?" Tim asks.

"You know that might not be a good idea now that the goal has been met. It might be better for both of us if we never meet. Wouldn't you agree?" Rosanne asks.

"Yes, I suppose you're right," Tim answers.

Before he can ask her name, she hangs up the phone.

The game against Edgemont High School begins poorly. By halftime, the score is Edgemont twelve Dobbs Ferry zero. Among the fans in the stands is Detective Anthony Pascutti. Anthony attends the high school football games most years, but this year he has been too busy, so this is his first game this season. He has always enjoyed basking in the village's school spirit and high school sports.

When the third quarter begins, Dobbs Ferry receives the ball and begins to march down the field by completing three consecutive passes.

"Looks like Coach Brown has lit a fuse under these guys," Anthony says to one of the fans. As the team marches down the field, the cheerleaders face the crowd and begin cheering, "Push them back! Push them back! Way back!"

In the center of the cheerleading line, Rosanne is holding a megaphone to her mouth, while she cheers.

Looking in Rosanne's direction, Detective Pascutti suddenly stops cheering. *A megaphone, I wonder if that might have been what the girl used that saved Joan Simpson from being raped?* He asks himself.

The Dobbs Ferry football team has been more than inspired by Coach Brown's halftime speech and wins the game forty-two to twelve, breaking a school record for the maximum number of points scored in a halftime.

On the way out of the football park, Anthony stops one of the cheerleaders and asks her how many megaphones does the cheerleading squad have. "One," the girl answers. "Only the cheerleader captain, Rosanne, has a megaphone."

When the team returns to the high school, Tim quickly showers, changes, and exits the school from the backdoor. He walks over to the practice field and leans on the fence, where he has a clear view of the aqueduct and the area with the huge maple tree. Tim remains standing in the same spot for some time in private thought. His moment of solitude is ended when an elderly woman touches him on the shoulder.

"Are you one of the football players in today's game?" she asks.

"Yes, I am."

"I just want to congratulate your team on such a fine game today."

"Thank you. I will be sure to tell them."

"I am here with a group of twenty other Dobbs Ferry graduates from the class of 1920. It's our fortieth reunion. I want to take a good look at this field, where I played girls field hockey forty years ago. I have done a lot of things in my life since then, but nothing has been more difficult, more demanding or as downright dangerous as going to gym class and playing field hockey on this field against the Dobbs Ferry High School women. The women in this village can be tougher than the men, and the men are tougher than most other men."

"I know exactly what you mean," Tim responds. "Nothing has changed in forty years."

Despite the enormous win, no one is interested in celebrating. The football game has lost its significance in light of what has happened to this normally peaceful village. There is no caravan of cars riding through the village, and no one stops at Sam's restaurant for pizza. The entire school is in mourning for Anna. Most of the students go directly home after the game, and get ready for the viewing of Anna at Edwards Funeral Home at 6:00 p.m.

The funeral home is filled with people within minutes after it opens. Mr. and Mrs. Rossi greet each person who pays their respects to Anna. In the entranceway, Detective Pascutti waits for Rosanne.

When she arrives, he does not address her. He waits patiently until she leaves the funeral home, where he stops her on the sidewalk in front of the funeral home.

"Excuse me, Miss Carrero, may I have a minute of your time?" he asks holding his badge up so she can see it.

"How can I help you?" she asks.

"Did you know Tito Menetti?"

"No, not really!"

"What do you mean, not really?"

"Everyone in the village knew who he was. He was a creepy guy, and everyone stayed away from him."

"Did he ever try to attack you?"

"No. Why would you ask me that question?" she asks slightly shaken. "Am I a suspect?"

"No, why would you think you're a suspect?"

"I have had enough of this. That poor girl inside is being buried in two days. Tito raped and killed her, and you're worried about who killed him. You must be the only one in the village who cares who killed him."

"I'm only doing my job, young lady. By the way, have you ever owned a bracelet like this one?" he asks, holding up the bracelet found in Tito's dresser drawer.

"Yes, I'm wearing it right now," she responds, while holding out her arm.

"I have to go now. If you need to talk to me, call my home," she says after she opens the door to her car.

"I may need to do that," replies Detective Pascutti. "The next time I may want you to come to the police station, where you will be more comfortable and maybe a little more cooperative," he says before her car pulls away. Detective Pascutti's short interview has convinced him that Rosanne is a person of interest.

Rosanne can't believe that Pascutti has begun to focus on her. *What got his attention? Has Tim been interviewed? Did Tim point blame in my direction?* she asks herself. *No, he couldn't have. He doesn't know I'm the one who called him. How did Pascutti narrow his focus on me this quick? I cleaned the murder scene of any remaining evidence. Shit! What have I missed? Oh think! What did I miss? Maybe he is just probing. I have to be calmer the next time.*

Chapter 28

It Will Be With Me Until I Die

Tim wakes up early Sunday morning. He dresses and leaves the house before anyone else is awake. He arrives at the golf course about the same time as Father John. They sit down next to one another. Father John spends the next fifteen minutes analyzing the world and its problems. Tim doesn't appear to be as attentive as he usually is.

"Something bothering you today, my boy?" Father John asks.

"Do you mind if I ask you a question related to the war? I know it's not something you like to talk about."

"If it will help you with what it is that's bothering you, I might make an exception."

"Did killing the enemy have any lasting impact on you?"

Father John stares directly at Tim without speaking. Tim stares back without moving or speaking. After a long period of silence, Father John shakes his head and begins to speak in a low voice.

"A lot of the fighting was upfront and personal. On occasions, it was hand-to-hand combat. Killing is against everything we were taught from when we were born until we entered the army. When you see the life run out of a man that is two feet away and staring you in the eyes, it becomes imprinted on your brain. It never leaves you. I can be watching a beautiful sunrise, or I may be fast asleep when one of those faces flashes in front of me. It will be with me until I die."

"Thanks," Tim says in a gloomy tone after another long silence.

"You aren't in any trouble, are you?"

"No, I'm not. I'm concerned about someone I know. I don't feel much like caddying today. I'll see you around, Father John."

"God bless you, son."

Tim walks up the first fairway without making his usual gestures of good-byes to everyone. When he exits the golf course, Johnny Pacetti appears directly in front of him.

"Hey, Johnny. How are you doing?"

"I'm okay," he says with a smile.

"How did you get that long cut on your neck?"

"I'm okay!"

"You can tell me, Johnny. I won't tell anyone."

Johnny looks around nervously before he says anything.

"Marco cut me with his knife. He has a gun. He held the gun to my head, and cut my neck. He told me to get him some caddying money, or he will hurt me."

"Where is Marco now?"

"I don't know! I don't know! Don't say anything to him. He will hurt me."

"Yeah, I guess he will. My lips are sealed."

"Do you know that Tito is dead?" Johnny asks.

"Yes," replies Tim. "Well, thank God he's not going to be bothering you anymore."

"Tito was a bad man. A real bad man," Johnny replies.

"Try your best to avoid Marco. Don't go down to the village where he hangs out or in the woods near the aqueduct," responds Tim

"I like to go in the woods near the aqueduct to get Indian arrowheads."

"For God's sake, Johnny, don't go near the woods! Marco will be waiting for you and will take your money or possibly hurt you. I have to go now. Enjoy your day."

"You too, Tim," Johnny responds after he takes a deep breath and his eyes open wide.

"Where is your yellow belt? I guess it's not a yellow day today?" Johnny asks.

"No, I guess it isn't," Tim responds before he departs.

Chapter 29

No Time to Say Good-bye

On Monday morning Anna's burial is attended by a huge number of mourners, including relatives, friends, high school students, and Detectives O'Neil and Pascutti. All of them want to pay their respects to a girl that represented the best that the village had to offer.

When Tim enters the viewing room, Rosanne follows not far behind him. She wants to observe him to see how he is handling the pressure of the police being ever present.

While Rosanne is following Tim, Detective Pascutti is following Rosanne. He wants to see if she has any lengthy conversations with anyone or spends time with any other person of interest.

Rosanne joins Tim when he greets Anna's mother. Detective Pascutti moves up close behind them.

"Thank you for coming. I appreciate your call the night Anna was missing," Mrs. Rossi says as she reaches out to gently hug Tim. Despite some background chatter, Detective Pascutti hears her greeting.

"I heard Tito was responsible for her death, and he is dead," Rosanne replies before Tim can speak.

"Yes, we have heard from the police that Tito was responsible."

"I'm going to miss her," Rosanne responds as she leans on Tim.

"Thank you for your concern," replies Mrs. Rossi. "We are all going to miss her. I wish we had time to say good-bye to her."

Rosanne turns before she leaves the greeting line, and realizes Detective Pascutti has been standing directly behind her. After Tim completes his condolences, Rosanne and Tim remain in the viewing room for sometime until Dino arrives. Dino joins Rosanne, and Tim leaves for home. Observing their body language, it is clear to Detective Pascutti that Dino and Rosanne are very attracted to each other. When Rosanne realizes Pascutti is observing every move she makes, she asks Dino to leave with her.

As she is about to leave the funeral home, one of the cheerleaders, Diane Gallente, asks her if Detective Pascutti had contacted her about her megaphone.

"No, he didn't," she responds.

"He wanted to know how many megaphones the cheerleading squad owns. I told him one, and you are the only one who uses it," Diane explains.

Rosanne knows immediately why detective Pascutti has been focusing in on her and decides to prepare herself for the next meeting with the police which she expects to be coming soon. By 2:00 p.m., Tim, Rosanne, and Dino receive phone calls from the Dobbs Ferry police requesting them to appear at the station for questioning at 4:00 p.m. on Tuesday.

Chapter 30

A Second Funeral

On Tuesday morning at 10:00 a.m., Edwards Funeral Home has a quiet viewing followed by a service and burial for Tito Menetti. In attendance are Tito's parents, some relatives, a few friends, and Marco Devito and Detective O'Neil. Detective O'Neil greets Mr. and Mrs. Menetti, expresses his condolences, and then asks Mr. Menetti if he can speak with him off to the side for a few minutes.

"Mr. Menetti, I know this may not be the best time to ask you questions, but what I have to ask you may be helpful in finding out who killed Tito. Can you think of anything that Tito owned or would have had in his possession that is missing?" Detective O'Neil quietly asks.

"Yes, I'm glad you asked," responds Mr. Menetti. "Tito had a pellet gun that he always kept on him when he went out. It was something he would not give to anyone. If you find who has his gun, you probably will have found who murdered him."

"Do you have any wood stored in your house or garage?"

"No, I don't."

"That's all I have for now. Thank you for your help," Detective O'Neil responds.

Detective O'Neil remains until Marco leaves. He stops him in front of the funeral home.

"Marco, I am Detective O'Neil. I understand you were a good friend of Tito."

"Yes, I was."

"Do you know of anyone who might have had a recent argument or fight with Tito?"

"Yeah, Yeah. I know someone!"

"Who would that be?"

"Tim Ferrari."

"What exactly happened?"

"Tim has had it out for Tito for sometime. Tim asked Tito if he had anything to do with his dog missing. Tito said no and that if he found Tim's dog, he would tie it to the railroad tracks since Tim was acting like Tito caused the dog to disappear. Tim told Tito if he hurt his dog, Tito would pay for it. Then they just stared at each other before walking away."

"Thank you for the input. Marco," responds Detective O'Neil.

"No problem, Tim Ferrari has a hot temper. I wouldn't be surprised if he did this to Tito."

He wants to believe Marco, but he knows Tim and Marco have recently had an all out fight, and Marco lost.

Marco excuses himself, telling Detective O'Neil he has family business and is late. He has no real intentions of going home. He has in his possession Tito's pellet gun and a knife. He plans on hunting down Daisy before he returns home. He has spent the last three days trying to locate Daisy. He figures, if he finds her, Tito's pellet gun and his knife should be enough to put an end to her. His reason for killing her has changed from causing pain for Tim to paying tribute to Tito. He plans to leave the dead dog's remains on Tim's front porch.

After one hour of traipsing through the woods, he decides to go home. By now, he is deep in the woods between the golf course and village that is bordered on the east by the aqueduct and the west by the Hudson River. He decides to rest next to one of the many paths that seem to go nowhere before he sets out for the village. While he is quietly relaxing, he hears the sound of barking dogs in the distance. The noise gets louder and closer as he waits with his gun in one hand and a knife in the other.

Not more than twenty feet from Marco, a dog walks out onto the path followed by another then another. Marco is happy to see there are only three dogs in the pack, and the one in the center is Daisy. The other dogs are bigger than Daisy, but they are thin and look sickly. On seeing Marco, Daisy's tail lowers and her body lowers to an attack position. Her teeth are visible, and she is growling.

Marco lines up the sites of the pellet gun, aims at Daisy, and pulls the trigger. In the same instant, one of the other dogs lunges forward and is struck by the pellet, but the wounded dog continues the attack and Marco swings the knife out as the dog lunges at him. The knife strikes the dog in the chest killing it before it hits the ground. Daisy and the other dog retreat back into the woods. Marco chases after them, but he is no match for their speed, and they soon disappear in the woods.

While he is upset that he came so close to achieving his goal but failed, it is not a total loss. He has a better understanding of where to go to locate this fox-like bitch the next time he goes looking for her.

Chapter 31

A Shot in the Dark

Tim, Rosanne, and Dino all arrive at the police station at 4:00 p.m. on Tuesday. Detective O'Neil asks Rosanne to join him in his office, and Detective Pascutti asks Tim to join him in his office, while Dino remains in the waiting room.

Detective O'Neil wastes no time with Rosanne.

"Rosanne, you are here to answer questions relating to the felony death of Tito Menetti. You will be expected to answer each question to the best of your knowledge. I'm not interested in your comments, opinions, or advice. You will simply answer the questions. Do you understand?" *

"Yes, I do," responds Rosanne.

"You were seen with Tim Ferrari at the funeral today. Did he say anything that would lead you to believe that he has knowledge of who committed the murder of Tito or was possibly involved?"

"No, he didn't. He said nothing about the murder."

"Do you have any reason to believe he was involved?"

"No, I don't!"

"Did Tito ever attack you in any way?"

"No!"

"Were you in any way involved in Tito's murder?"

"No, and I don't know who it was that killed him."

"You just said, 'who it was who killed him.' Do you have any reason to believe a single individual murdered him?"

"No!"

* The Miranda Rights became law in 1968. In 1960, a detective did not have to read anyone their rights before questioning them.

"Can you tell me where you were at approximately 7:30 a.m. on the day of the murder?"

"I was at home. I was getting dressed for school."

"Is there anyone who can verify your being at home?"

"Yes, my mother and father."

"That bracelet you are wearing is one of the two you have bought at the same store in the last three months. Where is the other one?"

"I don't know. I lost it."

"Did you lose it, or did Tito remove it from your arm?"

"I don't know what you're talking about. I left it in a restaurant bathroom when I took it off to wash my hands. By the time I realized I left it and returned, it was gone."

"What restaurant are you referring to?"

"Sam's Pizza."

"Are you the only cheerleader on your squad to have a megaphone?"

"Yes."

"Do you ever take the megaphone home with you?"

"Yes."

"Were you the girl that stopped Tito from raping Joan Simpson?"

"No!"

"Did anyone else take the megaphone home in the last two months?"

"No, not that I know."

"Do you know what I think? I think you are lying. I think Tito did something to you. He may have attacked you or even raped you at the same location that he attacked the other girls. You were afraid to tell the police out of fear of retaliation from Tito, so you began monitoring the activities around the crime scene to prevent another attack on someone by Tito. You succeeded in warding off his attack of Joan Simpson, but you failed to help Anna. Guilt consumed you when you somehow realized Anna was dead. Perhaps you witnessed her murder or discovered her body before the police could. You recruited your boyfriend and possibly Tim, and the three of you acted as judge, jury, and executioner in the murder of Tito Menetti.

"We now have evidence that you were at the crime scene. You would be better off telling me now how all this played out. It's only a matter of time before we fit all the pieces together. If you cooperate, things may go easier for you with the District Attorney. If we have to pull it out of you, we're not going to go easy on you. Now, do you want to start all over again? Only this time with the truth."

"I don't know what you are talking about. I have told you everything I know. I want to go home now."

"You will go home when we have completed this interview. I can't imagine how you must feel if he has raped you. It's time to get all this off your chest. A jury is sure to show leniency under these circumstances. You will feel a lot better if you tell us what happened, and we can help you through this difficult time."

"I want to see my lawyer, and I want him available for any further discussion."

Detective O'Neil has taken a shot in the dark hoping it might lead to uncovering some information, or if Rosanne is indirectly involved in the murder, she may tell exactly what happened. The effort is not going well. She knows her rights, and without any evidence, he has no reason to detain her.

"Remain seated. I will get you some water before we discuss your right to a lawyer. For now, perhaps you can give some thought to what I have said." Detective O'Neil exits the room, so Rosanne can sweat it out a little. Five minutes later, he returns with Dino. "I want you to remain in the waiting room until I finish interviewing Dino. If you feel you need a lawyer, you can contact him now," Detective O'Neil directs Rosanne.

When Rosanne leaves the room, he begins the interrogation of Dino.

"Before we start, I want to make it clear to you. I don't want your opinions or smart remarks. Just answer the question, and we will get along fine."

"How long have you been dating Rosanne?"

"A little over a year."

"Did she ever mention she lost her bracelet?"

"No."

"Did you ever have an altercation with Tito?"

"No. Who would want to tangle with that guy?"

"Are you good friends with Tim Ferrari?"

"Yes, I would say we're good friends."

"Did Rosanne ever tell you it was Tito who attacked Joan Simpson?"

"No."

"Did Tim ever tell you it was Tito who attacked Joan Simpson?"

"No."

"Did Rosanne ever tell you that Tito molested or raped her?"

"No, of course not."

"Rosanne said she had told you that Tito attacked her, and she said you reacted violently, and you said you would take care of him. Is it true?"

"No, it's not true that I said I would take care of him, or that I did anything to him!"

"Did you or Rosanne get someone else to take care of Tito?"

"I came down here to answer your questions and be helpful, not to be treated like a suspect. I'm not answering any more questions until I'm appointed a lawyer."

"Don't get smart with me."

"I'm not getting smart with you. I'm telling you my rights. So unless you can get me a lawyer, I'm not answering anymore questions."

"Look, we can get you a lawyer, but it will only delay the process. One way or another, you're going to answer all our questions. So how do you want to proceed? You can be cooperative and continue, or you can act like someone who has something to hide and ask for a lawyer."

"I'd prefer to wait for a lawyer."

"Okay, we will pick this up again in a couple of days when you are able to have your lawyer available."

Detective O'Neil escorts Dino to the waiting room, where he tells Rosanne and Dino they can leave, but they will be questioned again in the future and to have their lawyers available.

While Detective O'Neil has been interrogating Rosanne and Dino, Detective Pascutti has been busy interrogating Tim. Tim is tight-lipped about every question asked of him. He makes no reference to the call he received from Joan's Good Samaritan and answers *no* to every question about being involved in Tito's murder. Before he is allowed to leave, Detective O'Neil joins the interrogation. He tells Tim that Rosanne is beginning to confess and that she is implicating him in the murder of Tito. Before he can ask any further questions, Tim asks for an appointed lawyer and wants the lawyer present before he answers any more questions. Detective O'Neil ends the interview and tells Tim he can leave.

If their demands are within their rights, the detectives have to respond to those demands or else whatever is said may not be admissible in court. However, if they don't know their rights and they allow the interview to continue, anything said can be used against them in court. Detectives O'Neil and Pascutti are not happy with the results of the interviews. Whoever is giving them advice on their rights is not making the detectives' job easy.

"All three of these students have asked for lawyers. Someone has prepared them for this interview," Detective O'Neil explains to Detective Pascutti.

"Yeah, someone has definitely told them to lawyer up if they think they are being considered as suspects," responds Detective Pascutti.

"Let's wait until we get a little more information before we take another crack at them."

"Dino looked surprised, even shocked, at many of the questions I asked him. He may not have been involved in any of this. On the other hand, I am certain Rosanne has had some form of involvement in Tito's murder. She is a tough kid. We've got our work cut out for us to get her to talk," explains O'Neil.

"Tim was hard to read. He seemed cooperative and responded to all my questions, but in the end, he said very little," responds Pascutti.

Before all three students arrived at the police station, at Boo's request, they had spent a half hour with a lawyer who belongs to the Royal Arcanum. Among the instructions he gave them was to ask for a lawyer if they think they are being treated as a suspect and to say as little as possible when answering questions. The people of the village support its own, especially when they believe proper justice has been carried out.

Chapter 32

A Thanksgiving Day Speech

T he following Thursday morning, the District Attorney meets with reporters to announce that the murder of Anna Rossi has for all intents and purposes been solved.

"There is a preponderance of evidence tying Tito Menetti to the crime and no further evidence that anyone else was involved," he begins. He lists all the evidence, including Tito's fingerprints and shoe prints at the scene of the murder, and his possession of Anna's bra, underwear, and earrings. Tito's possession of Joan Simpson's underwear shows evidence that he had previously attempted to rape someone else. The

District Attorney completes his meeting by saying, "Unless there is any new evidence that points to additional suspects' involvement in the crime, this murder case will be considered solved."

After a week of people locking their doors and not allowing their children out late or walking the aqueduct to school, the village residents begin to relax. By the end of two weeks, things seem to return to normal at least on the surface.

The football season ends with Dobbs Ferry's record at seven wins and one loss. There is much to celebrate although having a winning season doesn't seem to be as important as it had just two weeks earlier. Tim continues to date Joan, but no one mentions that he remains a suspect in the murder of Tito. Rosanne and Dino continue to date. Dino has asked her if she was in any way involved in the killing of Tito, and she has assured him she wasn't. Dino is satisfied she is telling the truth. As for Detective O'Neil's statement that Rosanne had implicated him in the murder, he has accepted it to be nothing but a ploy by O'Neil to get him to implicate Rosanne.

When Thanksgiving arrives, Tim and Joan have dinner with their individual families. Veronica invites Tim's elder brothers, Roy and Jerry, and their families. His sister Jane will be home from nursing school. It has been a while since they were all together. Boo surprises everyone by not disappearing and is in attendance at dinner. The dinner consists of everything a typical American Thanksgiving should have. The turkey is huge and cooked with tender loving care by Veronica and Roy's wife Millie. The Ferrari home is a large duplex. Roy bought half of the duplex from Boo four years ago and lives next door. A small prayer is usually given on previous Thanksgivings, so everyone is surprised and quiet when Boo begins a Thanksgiving speech that is far more than a prayer.

"I have had time to reflect on this year more than most others, and I realize we have much to be thankful for. This is an incredible country. I want to thank our ancestors for having the guts to leave Europe and for coming here with little more than the shirts on their backs and dreams of starting a new life. Our immediate family has had to struggle through the Depression and live off the generosity of others. We not only survived, but we were also able to buy this house going on seventeen years ago, and we are still here.

"Life is short enough as it is. This year, we have experienced a young girl's life cut short by circumstances we could not predict or control. I am grateful we are all alive and well. I am grateful we live in this special village, where something like a murder is almost unheard-of. I am thankful for being in a land where the law is fair, and an individual is presumed innocent until proven guilty. I am thankful for being an American. I am grateful for having this special woman for my wife and for this delicious meal." After a minute of stunned silence, Roy clears his voice and says, "Let's eat."

Chapter 33

Desperate Men Do Desperate Things

T he day after Thanksgiving, Tim, Rosanne, and Dino receive phone calls requesting them to be at the police station at 10:00 a.m. Saturday for questioning on the murder of Tito Menetti. Detective O'Neil has not turned up any new evidence, but he still wants another crack at the three students. They all arrive on time with their court-appointed lawyers.

Detectives O'Neil and Pascutti take turns interviewing each student. They ask the same questions they had asked in the previous interview, along with a long list of new questions. The detectives tell each student that the others have confessed and implicated the student being questioned, but the students remain tight-lipped, and at the end of the interviews, the detectives have gained no ground in uncovering who might be involved in the murder of Tito.

Tim returns home at 2:30 in the afternoon, and Boo is in the kitchen with Roy. They usually get together before a local carpenter's meeting to discuss the items on the agenda of the meeting. "Come in here," Boo demands when Tim enters the front door. Tim walks to the kitchen half expecting a barrage of questions. "Sit down!" Boo demands, and Tim sits down at the kitchen table. "How did it go today?" Boo asks.

"They asked the same questions. They have no leads to who killed Tito, so they keep hammering the three of us. I guess they have nothing to do with their time?" responds Tim hoping that will end the questions.

Before Boo can ask another question, the doorbell rings while someone is viciously banging on the front door and yelling for Boo to come outside. It is one of the local carpenters. He hasn't been working for months and is drunk. Boo gets up and runs to the front door before Tim and Roy have lifted themselves out of their chairs. They aren't the least worried about Boo's safety. Boo has been through this situation many times. He keeps two chairs on the front porch for just such confrontations. Boo's two sons remain next to the front door in case things get out of hand.

Boo doesn't want to waste any time with this guy, who is more than twice his size, broke and desperate. First, he must get him to calm down before he listens to his complaints.

"I'm Jack Delaney, and I want you to take a good look at my face so you know who I am. I've been out of work for three months now, and no one in this union gives a shit or cares or seems to know who I am," the carpenter yells at Boo in a slurred voice while pointing a finger about two inches from Boo's chest.

"Jack, I will do my best to help you, but first, I need you to sit down in one of these chairs, so we can talk this out," Boo responds.

"Talk! That's all I get from you guys is fucking talk," Jack responds as he begins to pace back and forth on the porch. "I need work and now," he yells after stopping and bending forward until he is about two feet from Boo's face.

"Then shut up for a minute and sit in this chair or get your drunken ass out of here," Boo screams back in a commanding voice that he reserves for these situations. Both men stand inches apart staring at one another for a few silent seconds before Jack sits down in one of the chairs.

Boo's voice and demeanor immediately change as he sits down next to Jack. The men discuss Jack's problems in a much more civil tone. Jack feels he is not getting fair treatment by the union business agent often referred to as the delegate. The delegate is responsible for meeting with construction companies, identifying their job requirements for new construction, and assigning the carpenters for the openings. Boo immediately calls the delegate, Joe Alonso, and asks him why Jack has been without work for such a long time and what he can do to help Jack.

"Jack's skills were not sufficient for the recent available local jobs, but if he is willing to work in northern Westchester, I believe there should be some openings coming up for his skills next week," Joe replies.

"Can you make sure he gets one of those openings?" Boo requests.

"You got it, Bob," Joe responds.

"You're going to have to do some traveling, but if you give the delegate a call on Monday, he should have work for you in northern Westchester," Boo explains to Jack.

"I'm willing to travel. That's no problem," replies Jack.

"Jack, my door is always open to anyone who has a complaint. However, I must ask you in the future not to drink before you come here and talk to Joe before you talk to me." Jack thanks Boo and quietly leaves.

Roy and Tim have been listening to Boo's performance. "How does he keep from being taken out?" Tim asks.

"It's a combination of his instinct of knowing how much each guy can handle and the respect these guys have for him," Roy responds.

"Boo has a positive side that I often forget about. I'll do my best to keep that in mind the next time he goes over to the dark side," Tim replies.

Chapter 34

A Simple Suggestion

On the following Monday, The Royal Arcanum has its monthly meeting. In attendance is Detective Daniel O'Neil. A five-year member in good standing, his friends know him as Dan. Before the meeting begins, Dan is asked to meet in private with Bob Ferrari and Louie Miller.

As Dan is being seated, he comments, "If this has anything to do with the investigation, you know I can't discuss it with you." Boo pauses and responds, "It is about the investigation, but we are not going to ask you about any of its details."

"Dan, we don't want to tell you how to do your job, but it does seem you have focused on three students and have not looked in any other direction," adds Louie Miller.

"No disrespect, Bob, but don't you have some self-interests here?" responds Dan.

"Yes, I don't deny it. I owe it to my son to be here. Dan, we're not telling you to do anything other than open your range of investigation."

"It sounds to me like you are trying to tell me how to do my job."

"It is not our intention to tell you how to do your job. We are simply suggesting you have a wider focus at this stage of the investigation."

"I have to respect you guys for your concerns. Your hearts are in the right place, and I'll do my best to keep an open mind to your suggestions. However, you must understand that if future leads or evidence points in the direction of any of these three kids, then I'm going to do my best to get to the bottom of exactly what happened, and I will present my findings to the District Attorney."

"We fully understand your position and would expect nothing less of you. We know you well enough to realize you will do your best to do the right thing," replies Boo, while he stands and firmly shakes Dan's hand.

When Detective O'Neil leaves the room, Louie Miller asks Boo, "Do you think he had even a small change of view before he left this room?"

"Yes, a very small change. Although a small change embedded in your mind can act like a seed in the soil. In time, it can change your view of the world. We can only wait to see if our words had any impact on him."

"Bob, I hope for your son's sake that's true. Dan does not appear to be a man who easily changes his point of view."

Chapter 35

A Christmas Story

On the first snow day of December, Tim calls Joan and asks her to be ready for a trip to the woods and to dress appropriately. Tim arrives at Joan's house at 9:00 a.m.

"Where are we going?" Joan asks after she enters his car.

"On a Christmas adventure," responds Tim. Tim drives his car only a few blocks, and then parks adjacent to Masters School, a private girl's school, on Villard Hill.

"We're not allowed on the school's property," Joan advises.

"No, but we can walk up the hill a little, enter the school grounds from the back side, and make our way down to the woods behind it," explains Tim.

Tim opens up the trunk of his car and pulls out a saw and a sled.

"Are you planning to cut down a Christmas tree?" asks Joan.

"Not exactly," responds Tim. Tim leads Joan through a yard above Masters School, down past the back of the school, and just beyond the school's tennis courts.

"Life with you is always an adventure," exclaims Joan as her legs begin to tire from walking through the snow.

A short distance beyond the tennis courts, Tim tells Joan to sit down on the sled and hold on tight. He gets behind the sled and begins to push. The ground has a mild slope and Joan is enjoying the ride when Tim jumps onto the back of the sled behind her and puts his arms around her waist.

"You better hold on tight," Tim repeats. "There is a hilltop directly ahead."

"Oh, no!" Joan screams after the sled goes over the top of a steep hill and immediately picks up speed. The sled bounces off several mounds as it flies down the hill. Just before they reach the bottom of the hill, Tim shouts at her to let go and pulls Joan off to one side of the sled. The two riders tumble off together into the snow while the sled, with the saw tied behind it, speeds ahead and is stopped by a tree at the bottom of the hill.

"You are insane," Joan shouts at Tim who is still holding on tight to her.

"There is a reward for what you have just done," replies Tim.

"Oh really, what could that be?" Joan asks after she gently wipes the snow from Tim's face and kisses him.

"I guess the kiss is my reward, but your reward is off to your right."

Joan looks up to her right and gasps. In front of her is a straight path into the woods, and both sides are lined with white birch trees. The snow covered trees glisten in the sunlight creating a magical winter scene.

"Oh, Tim how wonderful! This is so beautiful," Joan shouts out as they walk in the direction of the path after Tim retrieves the sled and saw.

"This village is full of small treasures, isn't it!" Joan says with a sense of awe.

"No question about it. There are many hidden places like this in the village. You just have to know where they are and when is the best time to visit them. This site loses it magic when the snow is gone, but if you return in the spring, you can find Indian arrowheads almost everywhere you look," responds Tim.

"This should only take a few minutes," Tim explains as he walks a few feet into the woods and cuts off a branch of a white birch tree. He has chosen a good size branch that is five inches in diameter. He cuts the branch into five separate foot and a half long pieces and cuts ten two-inch long pieces from the thin ends of the branch. He pulls rope from his jacket then ties all the wood together into a bundle and ties the bundle to the sled.

"Okay, what is this about, mystery man?" Joan asks.

"We're going to make candelabras for your family and mine. We will have a few left over that we can sell, and we can use the money to buy each other a Christmas gift," responds Tim.

"We can't possibly walk back up that hill. How are we going to get home?" asks Joan.

"We are just a short way from Walgrove Avenue which will take us back to Ashford Avenue and the village. It shouldn't take more than a twenty-minute walk to get back to the car. Before we leave here, we need to find some pinecones and cut some small branches off a pine tree to use to decorate the candelabras."

After walking a little further into the woods, Joan collects some pinecones, while Tim cuts off small pine tree branches and manages to bundle them together, along with the pinecones, and attaches the bundle to the sled with the remaining string. When they return to the path, they can hear sounds of something moving in the woods, a short distance down the path. Tim looks back down the path as several dogs enter the path, and one of them is Daisy. "Oh my God, it's Daisy," he shouts. "Daisy! Daisy, come over here!" Daisy pauses, and then quickly runs back into the woods, along with her companions. "Wait here," Tim yells to Joan as he runs up the path to where Daisy has reentered the woods. He considers following her, but realizes the snow will make it impossible to catch up with her. He returns to Joan and explains that Daisy has been missing for months.

"At least I know she is alive. We have been looking for her down in the woods by the river where other people have said they have seen her."

"Why would she be in the woods up here?" Joan asks.

"I don't know other than she is very familiar with these woods since it's not far from my home. She must be able to find food around here," Tim responds. "More importantly, why did she run from me? She has been very close to me all her life."

"Let's go after her now," responds Joan.

"No, these woods can be treacherous, and the snow makes the conditions even worse. I'll take you home and then come see where her tracks lead me."

Joan reluctantly agrees, and they make it out of the woods and down to Ashford Avenue. As they pass the Grand Union on their left, the edge of the woods can be seen on the top of a hill behind the Grand Union. When Joan looks up, she can see the three dogs at the top of the hill.

"They must be getting some of their food from the garbage cans behind the Grand Union," Joan explains, pointing to the dogs on the top of the hill.

Tim stands motionless. He can't believe he has seen Daisy twice in the last hour after looking for her for three months and never seeing her once. Before Tim can move, the three dogs charge down the hill; only, they are not heading in the direction of the Grand Union. They race by the Grand Union and approach Ashford Avenue about thirty yards east of Tim and Joan. They cross Ashford Avenue and enter the woods behind the Catholic Church leading back down to the aqueduct and the safety of woods by the river and golf course.

"Damn it!" yells Tim. "I might have had the chance to catch her where they were, but she seems to disappear when she is in the woods by the river. We have searched there a number of times and haven't found her."

After about a ten minute walk they reach Tim's car. Tim opens the trunk of the car and in it are the remaining tools needed to make the candelabras, along with ten candles. Working out of the trunk, they are able to complete five candelabras decorated with pinecones, two candles, and pine needles within an hour.

They place two of the candelabras on the backseat of his car, and carry the remaining three with them down toward the village. As they pass homes along the way, Tim stops knocks on the front doors and presents the candelabras to the prospective buyers. Before they reach the bottom of Villard Hill, Tim has sold all three for twenty dollars a piece. He hands Joan thirty dollars and says, "Let's go shopping," when he completes his last sale.

They take their time walking through the business district of the village, and are greeted by many shoppers who, with the first snow, have caught holiday fever and wish them a Merry Christmas. Joan is accustomed by now to being stopped by people Tim knows, but today the number of people stopping him seems to have tripled.

"Is there anyone in this village that doesn't know you?" she asks.

"It isn't that they know me so much. It's more like they know my family. We have lived here a long time, and we are a part of a group of families that know one another for three or four generations," Tim replies.

Suddenly out of a side road a familiar figure appears. "Tim Ferrari how are you? How is your sister Jane?" Johnny asks with a big smile after lifting his eyebrows and inhaling air. "Merry Christmas to you and your family."

"Merry Christmas to you, Johnny!"

"Joan this is Johnny Pacetti. Johnny this is Joan Simpson. Johnny is the town greeter and he knows just about everyone in town."

"Nice to meet you Joan," Johnny says, as he shakes her hand.

"Johnny what happened to your eye?" Tim asks when he realizes Johnny's right eye is black and swollen. "Did someone hit you?"

"No, no one hit me. I fell down. I have to go now."

Johnny quickly turns around and runs down the side street.

"I guess he didn't want to answer any questions today. That poor guy is always taking a beating from one low-life or another in this town. He is probably afraid of what they will do to him if he tells on them," explains Tim.

"He is so pleasant. Why would anyone want to hurt him?" asks Joan.

"I wish I could answer that. I guess he is just an easy target. He will get over it. He always does. The next time he sees you he will remember your name and know your date of birth. How he finds your date of birth is a mystery."

When they finish their shopping, they walk back to the car. Before Tim gets in the car, Joan stops him and holds on to him. "You know this day is one of the nicest Christmas gifts I've ever been given. I hope we have many more days like this in the future," she says while putting her arms fully around him. "I hope you find your dog before Christmas. It would make a great Christmas present for you."

After taking Joan home, Tim drives to the Catholic Church and parks his car in the parking lot. He is able to spot dog tracks immediately. They lead down an embankment and to a creek behind the church. Only they stop at the creek. The dogs had obviously remained in the creek as they headed toward the woods. Tim follows the creek for a while, but he can't find any tracks leading away from it. Tired and frustrated, he gives up and returns to his car.

Chapter 36

A Dog's Night

On the same day of the first snow, Marco waits patiently at home. While others are happy to be able to go sleigh riding or shovel snow, Marco is happy to wait until the afternoon. By the afternoon, he expects there will be plenty of dog tracks in the snow making it easy to track down Daisy and her remaining companion. At 3:30 p.m. when it begins to snow again, he decides to head back to the area in the woods where he had last seen Daisy. When he arrives at the exact spot on the path where he had last seen her, he can make out the tracks of several dogs despite being somewhat covered by the newly fallen snow.

At first, he follows their tracks further into the woods; then he reasons that the dogs will probably return to the path area like they had in the previous encounter, so he returns to the path and sits and waits forgetting it gets dark by 5:00 p.m. in December. By 4:40 p.m., the woods are starting to get dark, so he decides in ten more minutes he will give up the hunt. With only a few minutes remaining, he hears the faint sound of dogs barking, and a big grin spreads over his face. *I'll wait until they are a lot closer before I head in their direction,* he thinks while grasping his pellet gun. As the dogs get close, the sound of their barking gets much louder than Marco is expecting. He pauses for a minute, and then begins to run.

He runs in the direction of the aqueduct, fearing that he may not be fast enough to reach safety in time. His instincts are accurate. The pack of dogs led by Daisy has picked up his scent, and they total a number of twelve dogs. By the time Marco is a short distance from the aqueduct, the sound of the barking dogs is deafening. The dogs are only thirty yards behind.

Marco exits the woods at Tito's hangout and turns right. He has only to make it over the narrow part of the aqueduct where there is a forty-foot drop off the sides. When he makes it onto the aqueduct, the dogs exit the woods and have cut the gap to twenty yards. He turns to see how far they are behind hum. It is dark now. When he turns to look back toward the village, he cannot see that he has angled his direction to the side of the aqueduct and runs off the edge of the forty-foot embankment with a cliff-like incline. He tries to grab the sides of the embankment as his feet land on air. It is too late, and his body careens down the embankment crashing on a pile of boulders at the bottom of the aqueduct. His head strikes one of the boulders before his lifeless body rolls over face up. He is still carrying the pellet gun in his right hand.

Above, the pack of dogs has stopped the chase as soon as he went over the side of the aqueduct. By now, the newly falling snow has covered the shoeprints from earlier traffic. The only imprints in the snow are of the dogs leading out of the woods, and Marco's shoeprints going fifteen yards past the dogs' footprints and ending at the side of the aqueduct. The dogs turn and retreat back into the woods with Daisy still in the lead. As if by design, the snow stops falling when the last dog reenters the woods.

Chapter 37

Accidents Do Happen

The next morning, after two consecutive snowfalls, there isn't much traffic on Main Street. As the sun rises, a lone figure can be seen walking up Main Street. Brian Hanson rises early every morning for breakfast at a local diner before he goes to work at a real estate company on Cedar Street. Before he passes the aqueduct, he happens to look down at the snow-swept view. After admiring the winter's white display, his eyes catch a view of something that looks out of place for the pleasant scene. It is the lifeless body of Marco lying on top of several boulders with one hand grasping a pellet gun.

Brian turns around and runs back down Main Street to the police station. When he enters the station, he is out of breath and can barely be understood as he shouts, "There is a dead body at the bottom of the aqueduct."

Within minutes, police and detectives surround the area. Tape is placed across the entrance to the aqueduct before they make their way down to the body. Detective O'Neil is one of the first people to arrive at the scene. He removes the pellet gun from Marco's stiff body after checking to make certain he is dead. The coroner arrives soon after, and in short order informs Detective O'Neil that the deceased has died from trauma to his head. It appears he fell or was pushed off the aqueduct. While searching the deceased's clothes, Officer Romano discovers a knife.

Detective O'Neil asks Officer McEntire to go to the top of the aqueduct, stop all traffic from coming in either direction on the aqueduct and begin taking photos of all shoeprints leading up to the spot where Marco had fallen. The only snow tracks that exist are Marco's and the dog tracks. No one had entered the aqueduct since Marco's fall the night before.

The detectives compare the shoeprints in the snow to Marco's boots and they match. They cannot tell from the dog tracks if the dogs were chasing him or if the dogs arrived at the aqueduct after Marco had fallen. What seems clear is that the dogs had not caused Marco to fall since their tracks ended twenty yards before the spot where he fell. Given that there has never been any report of a pack of dogs attacking a human in Dobbs Ferry, they conclude the dog tracks are not related to the death of Marco, and his fall is ruled an accident.

Detective O'Neil temporarily leaves the accident site, and he drives to Tito's home where Tito's father verifies the pellet gun belonged to Tito, but he can't identify the knife as belonging to Tito. He then drives to Marco Devito's residence. No one is home, so he goes back to his car and retrieves one of the wooden boards from the maple tree, and he walks around the back of the house where he finds the garage door open. He can see that there is a pile of wood at the back of the garage. In the pile he finds a board of the same width and thickness as his board. He lays his board alongside the garage board. The color and the wood grain match. He takes both boards back to his car and returns to the scene of the accident.

On arriving at the site of the accident, Detective O'Neil reviews his findings with Detective Pascutti, Officer Romano, and Officer McEntire. "It appears we may have solved the Tito Menetti murder case with the accidental death of Marco. The evidence is all circumstantial, but it strongly points to Marco Devito as being responsible for the death of Tito Menetti."

"The pellet gun Marco had managed to hold tight in his hand after his fall belonged to Tito. Tito's father has told me that Tito wouldn't have given anyone his pellet gun. The knife Marco had in his possession appears to have a blade width that matches the width of the knife wounds to Tito's groin. The wounds measured three inches long, and the knife blade measures three inches wide. This morning I found in Marco's home a wooden board that has the same width, size, color, and grain marks as the boards that were nailed to the maple tree, where Tito was murdered and were used by the murderer as a means to climb the tree," Detective O'Neil explains.

"Where is the motive? What possible motive could Marco have? Weren't they good friends?" asks Detective Pascutti.

"Yes, they were friends. However, a number of people have reported seeing Tito slap and even punch Marco when they would argue or if Marco didn't do things to Tito's liking. A neighbor of Tito's told me the very morning Tito was murdered he had seen Tito knock Marco to the ground and put his hands around Marco's neck, while he held Marco on the ground. The neighbor was too far away to hear what Tito was saying, but he appeared to be very upset. Tito may have gone too far once too often, and Marco responded the only way he seemed to know, with violence," responds Detective O'Neil.

"So we are back to one person committing the crime," exclaims Detective Pascutti. "Let's walk through the crime scene once more, so we are certain it fits. Marco arrives at the maple tree before Tito. He nails the two boards to the tree, and then uses them to climb the tree while holding the hanging belt and rope over his shoulder. He ties one end of the rope around his waist and the other end of the rope to one of the holes in the belt after running the end of the belt through the belt buckle making a noose. Then he waits for Tito to arrive. Tito arrives, is distracted, and somehow Marco is able to slip the noose around Tito's neck while hanging from a branch of the tree, and then he jumps off the branch causing Tito to be lifted into the air where he remained until he choked to death. Marco then unties the rope from his waist causing Tito's lifeless body to drop to the ground. He cleans up the crime site, removing all shoeprints or fingerprints. When he is done, he stabs Tito three times in the groin for good measure," responds Detective Pascutti.

"It's possible, but why would he stab Tito knowing he is already dead?" adds Detective Pascutti.

"I don't know," answers Detective O'Neil, "Marco will take the answer to that question to his grave."

"Why would he risk contaminating the scene after cleaning up? The stabbing appears to be a form of sexual revenge," responds Detective Pascutti.

Despite some loose ends, the evidence against Marco is too strong to ignore. With apprehension, Detective O'Neil reluctantly opens his range of the investigation beyond his first three suspects. He presents his findings to the DA, and the DA is convinced that the evidence points to Marco Devito as being responsible for the murder of Tito Menetti. Within two days, the DA reports the findings to the public, and the case is closed.

Detective O'Neil and Detective Pascutti are not fully convinced that Marco was the only one involved in the crime.

The following day, when Tim passes Rosanne and Dino in the school hallway, they all hug one another, and then continue in the direction they were going without saying a word. The investigation is over, and they can return to their normal lives.

Chapter 38

Nothing Lasts Forever

After the New Year, Tim signs up for high school wrestling. He had been asked on previous years to join, but had not shown any interest in the sport. He loses the first four matches mostly because he has no idea of what he is doing. Despite the losses, he is not discouraged. For the first time, everyone he plays against is the same weight as him. Every offensive end he played against in football was at least 25 pounds heavier, and sometimes, they had as much as a 50-pound advantage. Almost everyone he has wrestled is weaker than him. The years of lifting weights has given him strength beyond most people his same weight. Even the all-county champion from Hastings is shocked when Tim slams him to the mat. Tim is pinned by the champ in the third period after spending most of the first two periods on his back. When he is pinned, the Hastings fans cheer. Tim thinks they are cheering for the champ. They are actually cheering for Tim. He is the first wrestler this season to make it to the third period.

By the fifth tournament, Tim has adapted to the sport, and between the wrestling skills he is quickly developing and his added strength advantage, he is able to win the remaining ten matches to complete the season with ten wins and four losses. Joan attends most of the home matches, and they continue their close relationship throughout the spring months.

Tim has not given up his search for Daisy. He searches the woods where he had last seen her a number of times, but he is unable to locate her. He waits by the Grand Union garbage cans on evenings and early mornings, but she never shows up. By now, he has nailed missing posters all over the village, but the few calls he receives don't lead to her discovery.

At the completion of the wrestling season, Tim is hired at a Carvel ice cream shop located in Ardsley, the next village to the east of Dobbs Ferry. It is a two mile walk each way. Boo often lets Tim use his car to go to work. It has an added effect of keeping Boo out of the bars when Tim is working.

Tim applies to a two-year college, Farmingdale State College, and is accepted into the commercial art program. He realizes he has to save money and get a state or federal loan to pay for his education. By May, he is working most nights and weekends to save as much money as he can for his education. He has been spending less time with Joan, but he looks forward to the small amount of time they have together each week. On a Friday night in May, Mike Campi stops at the Carvel shop after attending a junior class private party.

"Mike, what's going down?" Tim asks. "What brings you out? I haven't seen you for a while."

"I just left a junior class party. It wasn't much of a party, so I left early," he says hesitantly.

"Is there something you want to tell me, Mike?"

"Well, I thought you might want to hear this from me rather than find it out on your own."

"Joan Simpson was at the party, and she was not alone. She was making out with this guy in one of the rooms."

Tim couldn't believe his ears.

"You're not having fun with me, are you Mike?"

"I wouldn't joke about something like this. I know how much you care for her."

"Do you know who this guy is?"

"Yeah, some preppy guy from her neighborhood. I think he goes to private school."

"Thanks for the input, Mike. I've got a line of people out front, so I've got to get back to work."

Tim's mind is spinning. *If she is tired of me, why didn't she at least tell me? Why did she do it this way? She must know I'm going to find out. God, this is hurtful.*

He finishes work at 11:00 p.m. The walk home is helpful. He uses the time walking to try to better understand what has just happened.

By the time he reaches home, he realizes that he is far more committed to her than she is to him. However, he cannot fully comprehend why she would use such a cheap way of breaking the relationship. At first, he is certain her family or friends have pressured her to end the relationship. After some thought, he recognizes that she is a junior in high school, and he is about to graduate in a month. She had a good time, but she doesn't want her senior year in high school to be spent waiting for Tim to come home from college. They have been very close and their time together has been special, but it is time for her to break the relationship. It all makes sense, but Tim isn't ready to say good-bye. He has grown to care for her too much to let go.

He is tired when he gets home and falls asleep in his bed before he gets undressed. Suddenly, someone is shaking his shoulder.

"Tim! Tim! Wake up," Jane Ferrari says while pulling at his sleeve.

"What are you doing here?" he asks.

"I just returned from nursing school this afternoon. Tim, where is Boo's car? It is not out front." Jane says in a low voice.

Tim jumps up, "Oh shit! I left it at work and walked home. Is there anyone around that can drive me there?"

"It's your lucky night. Carl and Mary Jane came over to visit me, and they are still downstairs. I'm sure he will drive you back to work. Go quick before Boo notices," responds Jane.

By Monday morning, Tim has thought through what he will say to Joan to avoid being mad, but when Joan appears down the hallway his emotions take control, and he cannot stop himself.

"Did you have a good time this weekend?" he asks as she approaches.

"Yes. I enjoyed this weekend," she replies

"How was Friday night at the junior class party?"

Joan pauses and isn't able to respond to the question.

"Well, I hope you have good time next weekend and the weekend after that and the following weekend during the Senior Prom. Have a good night then too. I've already asked someone else to go with me to the Senior Prom. While you're at it, have a good life!"

"Oh Tim, we need to talk."

"Actions speak louder than words," Tim responds while he walks down the hall leaving her behind.

Tim arrives home after working another night at Carvels. When he enters the house, Veronica is still up. She has been waiting for Tim to return home.

"How did it go today, Tim? Did you work things out with Joan?"

"Not really, Mom."

"Well, what did you say to her?"

"I guess you can say we parted ways."

"Tim, I know Joan has meant a lot to you. If you have to end this relationship, you must try to find a way that you both can walk away gracefully."

"I'm afraid it's a little too late for a graceful ending, and I'm not the one who has walked away. Let's face it, Mom. Sooner or later, she is going to meet the father of this family, and there is a high probability he will be wasted. I doubt she wants to miss going out dating and partying in her senior year. It is best it ends now. By taking someone else to the Senior Prom, I'm making the transition easy for her."

"You may be making it easy for her, but it doesn't sound like you are making it easy for yourself."

"Do you remember Jan Degeare? She is the girl that moved to Scarsdale. I have already called her, and she is going to the Senior Prom with me. If you remember what she looks like, you must know I am making it very easy on myself."

"Jan is a sweet girl, and she is no doubt one of the best looking girls you have dated, but the direction you are taking is still not in your interest. I think you should give it a little more thought on how to end your relationship with Joan."

Tim takes Jan Degeare to the Senior Prom and spends most of the night thinking about Joan. With two weeks left before graduation, he calls Joan and asks if they can meet. He picks her up after school. They sit in his car and try to work things out. Tim invites her to his senior graduation party at the Beacon Hill Country Club. They both agree to forget what has happened in the past month, and they will do their best to enjoy their remaining time together before he goes to college.

The graduation ceremony is flawless. There are speeches about the future and endless congratulations, hugs, kisses, and crying. When the ceremony is over, the students head to the Beacon Hill Country Club, where the real fun begins.

Tim drives to Joan's house and picks her up. They drive to the country club and change immediately into their bathing suits. The country club has a beautiful old building left over from the Levy estate and an Olympic-size swimming pool. Tim spends a few minutes in the pool with Joan before one of Joan's friends pulls her aside, and Tim soon finds himself alone.

After twenty minutes by himself, Tim decides he can use a drink. Many of the students have hidden bottles of liquor along the fence behind the bushes that line the property, where they can't be seen drinking. He walks behind the bushes and sees an array of bottles lining the fence, making what appears to him to be an open bar. He has never drank hard liquor, but there is a first time for everything he decides as he lifts one of the bottles, unscrews the top, and takes a good swig from a bottle of whiskey. It doesn't taste too bad, so he takes two more swigs. The third swig is more like a long gulp. He looks back at the bottle, and he realizes he has downed almost half of the bottle, so he takes one more swig for good measure.

"I better get something to eat before this stuff hits me," he decides, and then walks back toward the bathrooms. By the time he reaches the bathrooms, he is drunk, and on seeing Bill Moretti's large frame in the doorway, he tells Bill to step aside. Bill doesn't move fast enough, so with a drunken laugh, Tim throws his sneaker at Bill. The sneaker hits Bill hard enough to leave an imprint of the sneaker on his stomach. Bill wrenches from the pain and shouts out, "Sometimes you really piss me off, Ferrari," while he pulls the paper dispenser off the wall to avoid hitting Tim.

The following morning at approximately 10:45 Tim opens his eyes. He is lying face down on his living room floor. His throat is sore, and he can hardly speak.

"Hello, is anyone here?" he asks in a hoarse voice.

"My God, he is finally conscious," he hears someone say from behind him.

"Mom, is that you?"

"Yes, it is. Can you tell us what happened to you?"

"Right now you probably know more than I do. The last thing I remember was being at the graduation party."

"Bill Moretti brought you home last night after he took you to the hospital. You were drunk and tried to leave the party by climbing over a metal fence and got your hand cut on the top of the fence. They put three stitches in your hand at the hospital. When you arrived home at about 10:00 p.m., you were unconscious and your skin was a bluish tone. We tried to wake you, but you were out cold. Tim, what did you do? How could you get that drunk that fast?"

"I drank about a half a bottle of whiskey in less than five minutes on an empty stomach."

"Why would you do that?"

"I guess I am trying to end my relationship with Joan."

"Well, you succeeded at that last night."

"If you don't mind, I don't feel like talking any more. I need some time to think."

A minute later, Boo stands over Tim and kicks him lightly on the side.

"Get up and get yourself together," Boo demands.

"Give me a minute or two. I'm barely awake," responds Tim.

"All I have to say to you is this. You may be a football player and a wrestling star, but you will never be a man until you learn how to hold your liquor. Now get up."

Tim stands up, and Boo stares at him with a look of disgust for a few seconds. Then he shakes his head and leaves the room.

"Am I missing something here, Mom? Talk about denial! The man is in total denial!"

"Tim, he is trying to give you some fatherly advice," responds Veronica.

"Well, maybe, since I pulled his drunken ass out of his car last week, his timing is off. I'm sorry, Mom. I don't mean to upset you. I guess I've done enough already. I just need to find my bed and lie down for a while."

He manages to find his bed and goes back to sleep with just one thought on his mind; *How easy it was to make the same mistake Boo has made for years.*

By 1:00 p.m., Tim is awake. After a hot bath, he gets up enough courage to call Joan. To his surprise, her father lets him speak to her.

"I just want to tell you I'm sorry for what I just put you through," Tim begins.

"I'm sorry things had to end this way, Tim. My parents don't want me to go out with you anymore. I think it's better we don't see one another. I wish you all the best in the future. Good-bye, Tim," Joan responds, and hangs up.

Chapter 39

I Need a Job

For two days, Tim walks around in a fog. He soon realizes he will have to put aside his feelings for Joan and focus on getting a job for the summer. He has received a loan from the state to help him pay the cost of attending college, but it is not enough to pay all the bills. He must save $850 this summer and work in the college cafeteria to cover the remaining costs. He quits his job with Carvel. The pay is too little and they only want him to work part-time. Boo should be able to get him a job as a carpenter's apprentice during the week, and he will find weekend work for added support.

While Tim is developing a summary of his costs for Boo, Boo is outside tending to his vegetable garden. Boo's summer garden was once equivalent to a mini vegetable farm. Before the houses to the right of his property were built, he was able to use a quarter of an acre of the land to plant vegetables. Two blocks away, on the Levy estate, Mrs. Levy allowed him to grow corn on another quarter of an acre until her estate was sold, and a construction company built the Beacon Hill apartments on the site.

The vegetable garden provided the Ferrari family with a wide variety of fresh delicious vegetables every summer for years. In addition to his vegetable garden, he grew peach trees, grapes, and sunflowers along the sides of the house. The fresh vegetables made every summer meal taste pure and wholesome. The peach trees that he planted, by digging two large holes then placing a peach pit in each hole before filling them with ashes, rusty nails and dirt, produced large juicy peaches that everyone enjoyed. Now, his garden has been reduced to a small area in the backyard. It is a hobby that brings great joy to Boo. He will spend endless hours all summer tending to the garden.

From his bedroom window, Tim can see Boo is busy preparing the garden soil for planting. *I wonder what his life would have been like if he had become a farmer,* he asks himself as Boo happily continues to till the soil unaware he is being watched. *I don't know if he would have made much money, but he sure as hell would have been content as a farmer,* Tim assures himself. *On the other hand, I don't care for farming, so maybe I'm lucky he didn't become a farmer. Now, carpentry is something I'm sure I can appreciate and understand. I can't wait to get to work as a carpenter apprentice,* Tim thinks with anticipation.

During dinner, Tim begins to lay out his summer goal with Boo. After announcing his state loan application was accepted, he outlines what costs remain.

"All I need is a carpenter's apprentice job for the summer to help reach my goal of $850," he explains to Boo.

"Well, I'm sorry, but I won't be able to get you an apprentice job," Boo responds.

"Why, aren't there any openings this summer?"

"There are openings this summer, but each opening must go to a young man whose goal is to become a carpenter. I can't get you an apprentice position when your goal is to attend college. I'd be taking another young man's livelihood away from him."

Tim sits silent for a moment. "Are you joking? I need a job, and I'm your son. I'm not asking you for money. I know you can't afford to send me to college. I'm simply asking for work, so I will have a future. Doesn't your family come first?"

"Don't ever question my loyalty to my family. This is not about family. It's about the right and fair way to run a union," Boo responds in a raised voice.

Tim is stunned and quiet. Arguing with Boo won't change his mind. Arguing will only cause him to strengthen his position. Tim will have to look in another direction for a summer job.

Chapter 40

A Job as A Scab

Tim tells his older brothers of his dilemma and asks for help. Two days later, his brother Jerry, a banker, has a job for him, and they meet to discuss the opportunity. Jerry and Roy both have red hair and look more Irish then Italian. That is probably the only thing they have in common. Roy is quiet, loves to read, and enjoys spending hours by himself. Jerry is outgoing. He doesn't read much more than the newspaper and loves to have people around him. Because he is so outgoing, he makes a lot of friends.

"Tim, here is the phone number of the owner of a small construction company. The owner's name is Clyde. He is from the South, has a thick southern accent, is hard to understand, and can be difficult at times, but overall he is a good guy. He is a customer at my bank. He told me he is looking for someone to help cleanup after the carpenters and masons. It's not a big paying job at $2.25 an hour. If you do a good job, maybe he'll give you a raise. Only one thing, his workers are nonunion. If Boo gets wind that you are working for Clyde, he will have a fit. God knows what he will do," Jerry says with an expression of concern.

"Who cares?" replies Tim.

Tim follows up on the lead and is able to land a job with Clyde's Construction Company. In the first week of work, he hustles and gets every cleaning and sweeping job done in record time. At the end of the week, Clyde asks him if he wants to work with the masons supplying them mortar and cement blocks. Tim accepts, and on the following Monday, he begins working with the masons building the basement of a new home. He wears a reddish orange shirt and grey pants because it is a brick and mortar day. The work is backbreaking, but Tim doesn't mind. He is not averse to cursing, but here every other word out of the entire crew is a curse. After a while it gets a little overbearing. Despite being called fuckup, fuck face, the fucking kid, etc., he soon gets used to it and focuses on the work. The other laborer on the job is older and gets $3.75 an hour. Tim figures, if he does a good job, Clyde is sure to give him a raise.

By Thursday, he is outperforming the seasoned laborer. On Friday, the temperature reaches 95 degrees, and the seasoned laborer collapses from sunstroke. Tim decides this is his opportunity to excel. He mixes the mortar and supplies the two masons with mortar and concrete blocks for the rest of the afternoon. By quitting time, 4:00 p.m., the basement is almost done. When Clyde arrives at the building site at 4:15 p.m., Tim asks if he can have a private moment.

"This is as private as it gets around here. What do you want?" Clyde asks in his thick southern accent.

"Clyde, I fed two masons mortar and cement blocks all afternoon in 95 degree weather. Your seasoned laborer, who makes $3.75 an hour, collapsed from sunstroke. I did my job and his job for the rest of the afternoon. I think if I'm going to do this type of work, it's only fair you increase my pay to $2.75 an hour."

"Why, you ungrateful shithead. You're lucky you got a job. You work up a little sweat, and you think you can try to squeeze me for money. Who the fuck do you think you are?"

"Fuck! Fuck! Everyone is fond of that word around here, so let me show you who the fuck I am," responds Tim. He turns and jumps back into the newly build foundation. "This is who the fuck I am," he says as he pulls one of the freshly cemented blocks off the wall. Clyde yells, "Get that prick and teach him a lesson." Tim pulls another block off the wall before the masons can get near him.

"I'm the fuck who just helped build this wall," he yells as he manages to escape the two masons and pull another block from the other side of the foundation.

"I'm the fuck that has been feeding these two goons these blocks in 95 degree weather," he screams pulling out a third block.

In a scene looking like out of a silent movie, he is able to pull eight blocks off the walls before they are able to catch him. While one of the masons holds him, Clyde delivers a punch to Tim's stomach. He has never been hit by such power before. The one punch has almost knocked him out. He tightens his stomach and closes his eyes in anticipation of a second thunderous blow when the other mason yells out, "That's Bob Ferrari's son," causing the man holding him to immediately drop him. Clyde is about to kick Tim, while he is down to finish the lesson when one of the masons puts his hand on Clyde's shoulder. With a stone-faced look, he shakes his head indicating don't do it. Clyde gets the point and backs off. Tim, holding his stomach, gets up and starts to leave the site.

During the Depression, Boo helped start the local carpenter's union. He has been president of the local union chapter for most of the time since the union's beginning. He is also the local delegate to the district council for the Westchester chapter of the carpenter's union. With these two combined positions of power, he has helped to improve the local carpenter's wages and to get them their first benefits. Boo had helped many of the carpenters to get back to work during the Depression, and many others to get their first job. The union men respect him and are extremely loyal to him. He is not connected to any mob and has never strong-armed anyone. However, if the word spreads that a scab contractor beat up on Boo's son, Clyde probably would have to leave the area for a while to avoid the retribution of the distraught union members.

"Where do you think you're going?" yells Clyde.

"Home," replies Tim

"You better get your sorry ass back here at 8:30 a.m. to help clean up this mess," Clyde demands.

"Fuck you!" replies Tim.

"That will be at $2.75 an hour of course," responds Clyde.

"I'll be here at 8:00 a.m., Boss," Tim yells back with a smile, while still holding his stomach.

As Tim exits the building site, Detective O'Neil is standing outside the premises.

"Tim, I just witnessed what happened in the past ten minutes. You have a hot temper when things don't go your way. I want you to know I am still certain that you were involved in the death of Tito. I can't prove it but that could always change. Until then, I'll be spending my spare time keeping an eye on you. Anyway, sooner or later that temper of yours will get you in trouble, and I will come looking for you. Enjoy your evening," Detective O'Neil says with a smile.

"Thanks! An enjoyable evening will add to the great day I've already been having," responds Tim with a forced grin.

Chapter 41

A Mid Summer Rest

By the end of July, Tim has spent most his summer working. He is in need of a break, so he takes a day off and calls in sick when some of his friends ask him if he wants to go crabbing. When the Tappan Zee Bridge was built, a cement barge broke loose during a storm and sunk a short distance north of the Dobbs Ferry dump, making it a great place to catch crabs. There is also a small, secluded beach adjacent to the barge making easy access to it from the beach. The only problem is the currents in the Hudson are strong, so you have to get in the water either south or north of the barge depending on the direction of the tide, and let the currents pull you toward it while you push a tire tube with two bushel baskets containing the crab nets placed in the center of the tire tube.

Tim has joined some of the members of the Dobbs Ferry graduating class for this summer outing. Bill Moretti, Mike Campi, Don Sandino, Frank Tulio, Nicky Trapiani, and Fred Kerry are among the crew of day vacationers.

The crew swim out to the barge with all their necessary crabbing gear and a half-dozen six packs of beer without any trouble. Most of them have been making the same trip for the past three summers. Fred, an all-around athlete, is an exceptional swimmer. With the river always being a challenge, Tim is glad he has joined them.

They start catching crabs within minutes after baiting the nets with chicken and dropping them off the roof of the barge. By the time an hour has passed, they already have half a bushel of mostly large blue claw crabs.

The seven graduates lay down on the roof of the barge after they all pop open a beer for a little R & R and to soak up the sun.

"Look at that view to the south of the Palisades, and how about the view to the north of the Tappan Zee Bridge. What a contrast of the old world to the south and of the new world to the north! Damn, this is truly God's country. It never gets old no matter how many times you see it," comments Tim.

"Now look at the shore. Right behind the north end of the beach is where Wickers Creek empties into the Hudson. That area was once the home of the Weckquaesgeek Indians. They were probably standing right over there on the shore when first Henry Hudson then the Dutch settlers sailed up this river," Fred explains.

"You're shitting me," responds Frank.

"I shit you not," replies Fred.

"Do you think they used wampum to trade with the settlers?" Bill asks.

"Probably!"

"So there must have been Weckquaesgeek warriors living in the wilderness by Wickers Creek with white wampum beads holding onto their weapons and women while watching the ships with white sails," Bill concludes.

"Without a doubt. They had to be worried the white warriors would wade ashore," responds Fred with a smile.

"The Indians were here for thousands of years before us, and they treated this land as a sacred gift from God. It was in pristine condition when the first settlers arrived. Look, what we have done to this river. It's a shame. We probably shouldn't be swimming in it," adds Nicky.

"I wonder what life was like for a Weckquaesgeek Indian our age?" asks Frank.

"Life must have been hard, but he had all this around him to hunt and fish in, and he was free as a bird," responds Nicky.

"Freedom! Freedom! Freedom!" Frank shouts while raising his arms stretched out to the sky and standing on the top of the barge roof.

"Did you guys know my father and my brother, Roy, helped build the Tappan Zee Bridge?" Tim asks.

"No, we didn't," responds Frank. "At least I didn't."

"Yeah, there were four guys killed, building the Tappan Zee, and two were only about thirty feet from Roy when they fell off the bridge. One guy fell with his legs open and the water split him up the middle when he landed. Roy hasn't been the same about heights ever since."

"Wow, you just picked up my day with that story," Frank responds.

"Why do you think we always catch so many crabs here?" Mike asks the crew.

"You think it might have something to do with the dump?" asks Dino with a smile.

"No, it's not the dump. It's where I get my chicken faces and roaster crowns that make the difference," responds Tim.

"Yeah, he probably gets them from the dump," adds Frank.

"Do you remember I used to put Daisy in one of the tubes and push her out here? She would stay here for hours with us," Tim comments. "Any of you guys see her or her pack of dogs lately?"

"No, but we sometimes hear them at night. The dogs must go hunting at night," Frank replies.

On shore about halfway up a hill overlooking the river within view of the barge is a small cave. Inside the cave are a half dozen wild dogs. One of the dogs, Daisy, is watching every move of the young men on the barge.

"I'm going to miss playing Dobbs Ferry football," Dino comments.

"What do you think was our best played game this year?" asks Frank.

"It's a toss up between Edgemont and Briarcliff," responds Dino.

"My pick is the Elmsford game," Frank responds.

"Elmsford. Why Elmsford?" asks Dino.

"Well, if you remember, we started our warm-up with a Zulu war chant, like we always do in practice. We didn't think about the fact that the Elmsford team is almost all black. They thought we were mocking them, so their only goal in the game was to beat the hell out of us, and they did just that. They weren't going to buy we were honoring the Zulu warriors. They sent me to the hospital with a concussion. They knocked out a half dozen other players, including Tim and you, Dino. Yet we still managed to beat them 13 to 12. My head is still ringing from that game. It can't get any tougher than that day and still win," Frank responds.

"Hey, what do you think of President Kennedy?" Mike asks.

"Ask not what your country can do for you. Ask what you can do for you country." I'd be willing to help clean up this river if this town will rent me an outboard motor boat, so I can catch some of the big bass that are further out in the river," responds Frank.

"He is already creating a good feeling about the country's future," adds Tim.

"I'm getting a good feeling about Jackie," responds Dino.

"Kennedy is only forty-three years old and is president. What the hell are we going to do with our lives before we get old?" asks Bill.

"I'm going to get a car and drive out to Chicago and join the Playboy Club that Hugh Hefner recently opened," responds Mike.

"You can't afford the 25 cents a gallon for gas to get out there," Dino says with a look of concern.

"Do you ever get the feeling we don't act or think like normal people our age?" asks Bill.

"Yes, I've given a great deal of thought to your question, since others have said that about us a lot. After some study, I realized that the problem exists mostly in the river villages—Hastings, Dobbs Ferry, Irvington, Tarrytown, etc. The answer is obvious, we have all swallowed some of the Hudson River water, and we all have the Hudson River Syndrome," responds Dino.

"Are there any known symptoms?" asks Tim.

"Yeah, you seldom have a serious conversation without it turning into meaningless chatter."

"Anything else?"

"Yeah, no matter what you do, you always wind up having a beer. A less obvious symptom is you become left-handed. Our class has more left-handed people than anywhere else on earth."

"How do you know you are having a left-handed symptom if you are already a lefty?" asks Tim.

"Asking ridiculous questions is one of the most common symptoms."

"Left-handed people are creative thinkers and would not consider my question ridiculous."

"Now this conversation is starting to sound like meaningless chatter, which means it's time to have a beer."

"I'm going to miss you guys, and I'm going to miss this village life," Tim comments as he picks up his beer with his left hand.

"Here's to crabbing on the Hudson," he says, and then everyone takes a swig of beer with their left hand.

"Here's to all the Dobbs Ferry girls," says Dino, and they all take another swig.

"Here's to our future," says Bill. Then they all have a third swig.

"If we keep having toasts, we won't be able to swim ashore," Mike comments.

"Here's to not drinking," Frank replies, and they all have another swig.

After filling one bushel with crabs, Dino and Bill are getting bored and decide swim to the beach. They dive off the side of the barge and swim on an angle toward the beach realizing the tide is going out and will pull them to the south end of the beach. By the time they swim fifty yards, the tide is going out unusually fast, so they try to swim directly toward shore. Five minutes later, they are still about the same distance from shore. They are getting tired, and the four or five beers they have had aren't helping. Growing exhausted, they are able to grab onto a log floating in the water, and they yell for help. Fred, the outstanding swimmer that he is, jumps in the water and swims out to them in Olympic speed. When he is about five yards from them, they are both exhausted and now are screaming for help. Fred yells out, "Stop swimming, and let go of the log."

"What do you mean let go of the log?" asks Dino.

"I mean this," Fred replies as he stands up, and the water is below his chest.

Dino and Bill stand up and walk to shore with the sound of laughter coming from the barge.

The remaining crew place the bushel of crabs in one tube, the rest of the gear in the remaining tubes, and swim ashore. They plan on cooking the crabs at Mike's house after they all go home and clean up. Mike, an excellent cook, has been talking about the many ways he is going to prepare the crabs since they caught the first two crabs. The entire crew is starving and can't wait to get to Mike's house to enjoy the feast. When they make it back to the train station parking lot, Detective O'Neil pulls up along side them before they can enter their cars.

"That freaking guy won't get off my case," Tim comments.

"Enjoying your summer, boys," Detective O'Neil asks.

"You can't get much better weather than we have had today," Nicky responds.

"There was a break-in at the Beacon Hill Country Club last week. Someone, late at night, went swimming in their pool and stole all the frozen pizzas out of the snack bar. We have a witness that says it was you, Tim. He said you went swimming with a girl in the pool, and you broke into the snack bar after your moonlight swim. You want to tell me her name."

"Why don't you tell me? You seem to know everything," responds Tim.

"All right, smart ass, get in this car."

"Are you making an arrest? Because if you aren't making an arrest, I'm not going anywhere with you."

To everyone's surprise, Detective O'Neil does not come out of his car and arrest Tim.

"You're skating on thin ice, and sooner or later you're going to fall in," responds Detective O'Neil before he drives off.

"What the hell was that about?" asks Nicky.

"I don't know. I think he just wants to keep me on edge."

"Well, he appears to be doing a good job of it."

"Yeah, so much for rest and relaxation."

Tim continues working for Clyde for the rest of the summer, and Boo never finds out that he is working nonunion construction. He also finds a few lawn jobs and is able to cut his clients' grass after 6:00 p.m. on weekdays.

He sees Johnny walking in the village occasionally. Johnny is now able to enter the woods without fear of being beaten or having his money stolen. He has found a number of Indian arrowheads that he likes to show to everyone.

On Wednesday nights, Gould Park plays old movies during the summer on a huge outdoor screen. Tim enjoys going to the Wednesday night movies. It's a chance to catch up with friends and relax. On several occasions Joan attends, and every time Tim sees her, he realizes he hasn't come close to getting over her. She is constantly on his mind, and he misses being with her, but he knows it is over for her. He doesn't want to make a fool of himself, so he doesn't give more then a nod or say more than hello when he sees her. Underneath, he is aching to be with her.

Chapter 42

Suddenly It's September

July rolls into August, and suddenly, it's September. Tim spends the first few days of September getting ready for college. He has saved close to a thousand dollars, has bought some clothes, and has begun drawing and painting in his spare time. He wants to eventually become a cartoonist, but a two-year degree in commercial art will do for now. Dino has also been accepted at Farmingdale State College. They have requested to be roommates in the dorm, and the request has been accepted. Classes begin on September 7. They will leave for Farmingdale on September 6. On the day before he is leaving, he can hear Veronica crying in her room.

"Mom, can I come in?" he asks.

"Yes, come in," she replies

"Are you crying because I'm leaving?" he asks.

"Yes, I am," she says in a weak voice.

"Mom, it's not going to be the same as when Roy or Jerry went into the army. I will only be an hour and a half away. I'll be home for all the holidays, summer vacation, and probably some weekends in between."

Tim sits down next to her and puts his arm around her shoulder.

"Mom, you will always be with me. You will be there whenever I show the better side of myself. When I am kind to others or accept them for who they are, you will be near me. When I'm forgiving to someone who has made my life difficult, you will be with me. When I have fallen, it will be your endless examples of determination and courage that will help me get up. When I find joy in hard work, it will be from all the times I watched you sing while you cleaned other people's homes. You see you're not ever going to be far from me."

"Tim, did you recently read, 'The Grapes of Wrath' for an English assignment?"

"Well, actually I watched it on the late movie show last spring. I took notes and used them to create a book report for school. Okay, at the very least, I was able to apply Steinbeck's way of thinking to my world, and my heart is in the right place. How did you pickup on it so fast?"

"I have read the book twice and seen the movie at least three times. Just about anyone who has gone through the Depression has done at least the same."

"Well putting that aside, did I still get to you a little?"

"Yes, you did. Sometimes, you say the most touching things, but if you're saying all this because you're worried I might be slipping into a downtime, don't worry. I'm just crying because you have grown into a young man, and I'm going to miss you. The lithium I've been taking has almost eliminated my episodes of depression."

"Mom, I don't think I will ever be able to put into words how I feel about you. You have been my mother, my friend, and my source of inspiration. Am I starting to hit home again?"

"Keep talking. I like what I'm hearing."

"You know, everyone in the family says that you always liked me the best. Do you think that is a fair statement?"

"No! I don't know why they think that, other than you are the youngest."

"Well, I don't think it's true either. They say that you always talk about me when you are with them.

What they fail to see is you always talk about them when you are with me." Tim replies.

"That is true. Isn't it?" Tim adds.

"Yes, it's true. "

"You have always treated us all the same. Haven't you?"

"Yes, I have!"

"But we do have a little something special going on. Don't we, Mom?"

"Yes, we do!"

They both sit laughing for a few minutes. Tim has mastered the art of getting his mother to laugh and to feel good about herself.

"Don't ever lose your sense of humor, Tim. It's the sweetest thing we have in life, the ability to laugh at the world and ourselves. Without it, the world is a sad place, and life becomes more of a struggle."

"Okay, today should be a happy day. Tomorrow, I'm leaving home for the first time to prepare for my future, so let's go downstairs, have breakfast, and enjoy the rest of the day."

When Tim is about to sit down to eat breakfast, Boo enters the kitchen. "I want to wish you the best of luck, Son. I know you will do your best," Boo says as he shakes Tim's hand. "Thanks Dad. I appreciate the vote of confidence." There is a long pause, and for a second, Boo looks like he is about to hug Tim. Boo steps back, and Tim is reminded that in Boo's world a handshake is as far as a man will go to show affection to his son.

Chapter 43

A History Lesson from a Villager

After breakfast, Tim decides to take one last walk around the village before he goes away. He takes his time walking down to the business district on Cedar Street recalling the many experiences of his childhood as he walks by each building. When he reaches the entrance to the aqueduct, he stops and sits on the wooden fence that separates the Cedar Street sidewalk from the aqueduct, where he can see the aqueduct path and Tito's favorite maple tree. He isn't there very long when his brother, Roy, walks up alongside him and sits on the fence next to him.

"I'm glad I caught up with you, little brother. I want to wish you the best of luck before you leave," Roy says as he shakes Tim's hand.

Roy Ferrari is ten years older then Tim. He made it through the Korean War in the early fifties, returned home, and became a carpenter like his father. He married his wife, Millie, before buying half of Boo's duplex home, and now lives next door to Tim. Roy is a quiet and private person, who loves to spend his free time reading about historical events.

"Thanks, Roy. This view of the aqueduct has always given me an uncomfortable feeling. Even before the recent murders that took place here," replies Tim with his eyes still focused on the maple tree.

"Are you familiar with the history of the aqueduct?" Roy asks.

"No, not really," he replies

"Did Boo ever tell you when great-grandpa Murphy was ninety-nine he pointed at the aqueduct and said many a fine Irishman died building that water tunnel?"

"Yeah, about a dozen times," Tim replies causing both brothers to laugh together.

"This aqueduct is actually known as the Old Croton Aqueduct. It took five years to build and was completed in 1842. It is 41 miles long and runs from the Croton reservoir down south of here to New York City. It supplied the fast growing city with desperately needed clean water. Many of the citizens of New York City were drinking polluted water and were dying of cholera and dysentery. New York City's lack of water also threatened the city's buildings. Without enough water, fires quickly spread in city neighborhoods. Over four thousand Irish immigrant laborers, who were paid 75 cents a day for their labor, built it.

"The existing residents, who had to give over tracts of their land to accommodate the aqueduct, didn't welcome the Irish. Farmers and real estate barons owned much of land around the aqueduct. The Irish were penniless and lived in huts or shanties along the work sites. They were viewed as less than human by the landowners. There wasn't a police force in the area to maintain peace and order.

"The deplorable conditions led to the early deaths of many of the workers, as well as many of their family members. Another cause of death was the use of black powder to help cut through rough terrain. Dynamite wasn't invented yet, and many of the workers died trying to work with the highly explosive black powder. Penniless, they were often buried in makeshift graves along the work sites.

"Resentment over the low wages and poor working conditions led to strikes. The men who led the strikes were more likely to die in construction accidents than the workers who remained silent. God knows how many remain buried in the aqueduct due to the suspicious accidents.

"These forty-one miles of the Old Croton Aqueduct are lined with the bones of the long forgotten Irish souls, who still cry out for justice that will never come. Maybe the uncomfortable feeling you are having is coming from those poor forgotten souls."

"How about the Italians? Did they ever work on the aqueduct?" Tim asks.

"Well, good question. The New Croton Aqueduct began service in 1891 and is triple the size of the Old Croton Aqueduct. It runs much deeper under ground and is a few miles to the east of here. Italian laborers built the New Croton Aqueduct and rebuilt the Croton Dam. The New Croton Aqueduct still supplies water to New York City. The Old Croton Aqueduct was shut down in 1955.

"While the work conditions were somewhat better for the Italians, there were still problems and prejudice that the Italian laborers faced. The New York Aqueduct Police maintained law and order at the construction camps during the building of the New Croton Aqueduct. Most the Italian immigrants were from southern Italy and were professional masons. The contractors set up rows of shacks for them to live in and paid them $1.25 a day. Things hadn't changed much for new immigrants in the fifty years between building of the old and new aqueducts.

"Many of the Irish and Italian immigrants that built the old and new Croton aqueducts settled in Westchester County after they completed their work. The Irish found work in the building and maintaining of the Hudson River Railroad. One of them was great-grandpa Murphy. The aqueduct's Irish immigrants led the way for the 1,500,000 Irish that came here between 1845 and 1855 during the potato famine. They eventually gained acceptance for their hard work, patriotism, and heroic actions in the Civil War. The Italians also gained acceptance for their hard work, their patriotism, and heroic actions in WWI and WWII. Many of our Italian and Irish relatives and neighbors have roots in this area that begin at the Croton Aqueduct.

"Another interesting group of people that have a history in the land going back long before our ancestors is the Weckquaesgeek Indian tribe, who inhabited Westchester County prior to the Dutch. Like many other tribes, their immune systems were defenseless against the foreign diseases that the Europeans brought with them to America, and most of them died, or sold off their land, or were forced to move North to the land of the Wappinger tribes within a century after the arrival of the Dutch. Their remains are buried throughout the county. Hell, they uncovered Indian remains on one of the lots behind our house when they built two new homes there about ten years ago.

"I am certain if the aqueduct construction crews uncovered Indian remains, they did nothing to preserve them. In all likelihood, the remains of the Irish and the remains of the Weckquaesgeek have been joined together forever in the grand effort to supply the inhabitants of Manhattan enough clean water to survive and grow.

"In 1626, the Dutch bought the island of Manhattan for sixty guilders, or $24, from the Canarsee Indians of Brooklyn. At the time, the rights to Manhattan belonged to the Weckquaesgeek Indian tribe. The Weckquaesgeek first had their southern land given away to the white invaders by a neighboring tribe. Two centuries later they had to suffer the indignity of having their northern burial grounds disrupted to provide water for the invaders growing metropolis, New York City.

"Indians lived on this land for four thousand years before the Dutch arrived. Maybe it's a combination of ancient Indian spirits and the lost immigrant Irish souls that walk the aqueduct path at night that are making you feel uneasy. To tell you the truth, I've always felt the same way about this stretch of the aqueduct.

"Tim, we all have taken advantage of what this village has to offer. Although, I have to say, I don't know many people who have reached out to every corner of this village the way you have. I don't think there is a square foot of ground in this village that you haven't stepped on or used to make some spending money. If you go chasing your dreams with the same energy you put into living here, you will make us all proud.

"We are the reason our great-grandparents got on a ship to take a chance on a new world. They wanted a better life and opportunities for their children, their grandchildren, and beyond. They were willing to accept any challenge or overcome any obstacle that was thrown at them. Some of them lived in shanties and squalor and were rejected and shunned by their neighbors so that someday the sons of their grandsons could dream the biggest dreams in a land, where anything is possible. With an education, you may have a life where your dreams come true and live in other parts of the country, but this village will forever be your home. It is the promised land of our ancestors.

"The Great Depression would have been seen as a minor disturbance to them. For many of them, the miserable life they first had here was actually a step up from what they had in Europe. Grandpa Murphy told me during the potato famine, the Irish farmers ate anything they could to stay alive. First, they ate their livestock, and then they ate their family pets, and finally, the mice, rats, insects, or anything that moved. In the end, many of the dead had green lips from trying to eat the grass to survive.

"Here, they had enough to eat. Here, they could find work. Here, they were able to practice their religion. Here, many of them lived long enough to see their sons or grandsons own a home. Many of the local residents, at the time, thought the Irish drank because they were penniless. They drank, mostly, to celebrate being in a new world, where anything is possible.

"Many of the wealthy New York transients in this town like to say the local villagers think they fall off the earth if they go past the buoy at the bottom of Main Street. What they fail to recognize is that we have what they are usually looking for, only they fail to recognize it, a place where there is everything we need and a sense of belonging.

"You have Dobbs Ferry blood in your veins. It is the blood of your Italian and Irish ancestors, who made many sacrifices for you to be able to live in this village. It will never let go of you completely. Try to keep that in mind when you are deciding where you are going to work and live after college.

"Tim, I didn't come down here only to say good-bye or to give you a brief lesson in local history. Before you leave, I have to ask you just one important question because I am your brother, and I am concerned about you. Your answer will not be shared with anyone."

"Go ahead. Fire away."

"Tim, were you involved in the death of Tito?"

"Roy, that is an unfair question. If I say no, you may still think I'm lying. If I say yes, I might be saying yes to put an end to the questioning. Either way, I can't win. Let's just agree that justice was served, no matter who did it."

"If that's what you want, I can accept your answer," Roy replies.

"It's too bad I can't get Detective O'Neil to think the same way."

"Why? Is he still questioning you about the murder?"

"No, but he is forever present. He shows up in more places then I can keep count of."

"He accused me of stealing from the Beacon Hill Country Club. He drove off when I refused to get in his car unless he was going to arrest me."

"It sounds like he is harassing you."

"Well, he hasn't laid his hands on me which surprised me."

"He is not likely to rough you up if that's what you mean."

"There were too many witnesses for that to happen now that I think about it."

"That's not the only reason he hasn't gotten physical. A few years back, we had an officer in town that thought he had to rough up some of the kids to get their attention. One night, some of the townspeople threw a blanket over his head to let him know that he is not above the law and warned him that his behavior is not going to be tolerated in this village. They called it a *Blanket Party*."

"Was it O'Neil?"

"No, it wasn't. The point is the officer was much more respectful of the citizens after receiving the notice, and I'm sure the rest of the police force heard about it.

"The Dobbs Ferry police have always been fair and sensitive to the citizens and their children. We have all received a small tap with a nightstick if we didn't move when we were asked to. Everyone in town accepts that as part of officer's responsibilities. Once in a while, some cowboy makes it through the police academy and decides he has absolute power over every kid on the street and starts cracking heads with his nightstick. The villagers will put him through a retraining session if it gets out of hand.

"I suppose that kind of thinking might go back to the building of the Old Aqueduct when there was no police force, and the Irish workmen had to band together to protect themselves from the constable and his self-appointed hooligans. Tim, if some of the local villagers believe you had taken the law into your own hands and were responsible for Tito's death, even though justice was served, you may be in danger of them delivering their own form of justice in return. Be careful what you say to people in this town. It is probably good you are going to college. It gives a chance for any remaining suspicions to fade.

"On another important subject, you don't have to worry about Mom when you're gone. Millie and I are right next door if Mom is in need of any help, and Jane will be home in between nursing assignments."

"Thanks, Roy, she does seem to be doing much better since her doctor started giving her lithium and stopped analyzing every family relationship she has had since birth. My biggest fear has always been they might decide to give her shock treatments again."

"No one is going to give her shock treatments again. You can rest assured on that! You can go to college not having to worry about that happening! Keep in mind that she always manages to make her way out of every episode of depression. She may look frail, but she can probably handle a lot more than we can."

"Thanks again. I'm going to miss everyone in the family and this village life."

Tim says good-bye to Roy and walks down Main Street to have lunch at the Shamrock House. Rick

Squilera is tending bar, and he wants to say good-bye to him before he leaves.

"Rick, how the hell are you?" Tim asks as he enters the bar.

"It ain't easy being Rick Squilera! How are you these days, Tim?"

Tim has gotten to know Rick over the last year, and they are slowly becoming good friends.

"Do you have everything packed and ready to go?"

"Not yet. I plan on doing that when I get home."

Rick pours two beers and places one beer on the bar in front of Tim.

"This one is on me, buddy. Here's to you, Tim and all the success at college. I have some good news about myself. I have just been accepted at Iona College, and they have given me a scholarship to make it easy for me to attend. I'll be majoring in English. Someday, I'm going to write a novel about growing up in this village."

"Why am I not surprised? Maybe it's because you can do those word jumbles in about a minute and a half without writing anything down. The fact that you have read more books than anyone I know, and you use your gained book knowledge to counsel half the people that come into this bar might be a clue.

Here's to you, Rick. It's been a pleasure getting to know you."

"Maybe leaving this area will get your mind off Joan, and you'll find someone new to spend your days and nights dreaming about."

"Very funny. It might seem funnier if it wasn't true."

"I was just testing you to see if that flame was still burning as brightly as the last time we spoke."

"Well, it is."

"I've been giving some thought to your situation. I believe I have a solution for your problem. When I net everything out, it is clear that you are more in love with her than she was with you. She has quickly moved on, making her less interested in you than she appeared to be."

"I can't disagree with that."

"Somewhere in the back of your mind, you think there is still a chance to get her back."

"That's probably true."

"Since she has no real interest in you, your only way of getting over her is to do something that will convince yourself that you don't have a chance in hell of getting back with her."

"Are you serious?"

"I am serious, as difficult or even ridiculous as it sounds."

"If you are still walking around in this dream world you are in a year or two from now, ask her out. She will probably go out with you out of curiosity. All you have to do is make an ass out of yourself all over again. Then you will know for sure you don't have a chance in hell with her, and you will be able to move on."

"Why do you give everyone in here sound advice and then come up with this crazy advice for me?"

"It only sounds crazy now. If you are still dreaming about her two years from now, it won't sound that crazy. The only thing I'm not certain about is how much in love with her you are. We know it's a lot. However, could some of the feelings you have for her be a form of escape from your real world, where you have the everyday stress of trying to live in a family that has some difficult problems?"

"Let's forget about Joan for now. Are you still going to be working here?"

"I'll be here on weekends and holidays. If there is anything I can do for you before you leave, speak now."

"There is one thing you can do. Here is a picture of my dog Daisy. I mentioned to you I was having trouble getting her to return home. Could you keep your eye out for her around the village?"

"She is a nice-looking dog. I have seen this picture of her on posters around the village. I'll tell you what

I'll do. I'll hang this picture of her behind the bar for everyone to see."

"Thanks, I appreciate the support. I doubt if she looks that healthy these days. I haven't seen her for at least three months, and she has been gone for almost a year. I've only seen her four times in the last year, and two of those times were on the same day. She has joined a pack of dogs that survive by eating out of the dump, the Grand Union garbage cans, and God knows where else. I have no idea why she wandered away. She was very close to me, and we took great care of her."

"Have you made many attempts to track her down?"

"I've spent time waiting at the dump and the back of Grand Union on a number of mornings and evenings. I've searched the woods by the river, around the golf course, and behind my house a number of times as well. The few times I got a glimpse of her, she took off like a bat out of hell."

"You sure do have trouble keeping your women. Don't you?"

"Hey, I was looking for a little support here."

"I was reaching for a little humor to cheer you up. I guess it missed its mark."

"Even if you happen to spot her, she is not going to let you near her. I just want to know if she is alive."

"Tim, I'll make sure everyone who comes in here sees this picture, knows she is missing, and knows you need our support."

"Thanks, Rick. I know I can count on you."

Rick serves Tim lunch, and the two newly found friends bid one another good-bye. Tim leaves the Shamrock House and heads back up Main Street in the direction of home. At the top of Main Street, he can see Detective O'Neil walking down Cedar Street, and he is walking directly toward him.

Oh shit, this guy is on the prowl again, Tim whispers to himself.

"Good afternoon, Mr. Ferrari. I thought it might be a good idea to catch up with you, and let you know that just because you are going to college doesn't mean I'm going to stop trying to uncover what really happened on the aqueduct last year. Someone got lucky when we found all the evidence that led to Marco, and I believe that someone was you."

"Isn't there a difference between the words investigate and harass? You know there is no such word as harastigate, but I think your turning it into a real word. Weren't you once invited to a *Blanket Party* for similar actions?"

Detective O'Neil turns bright red as his face contorts into a display of anger.

"It may surprise you to know there is no statue of limitations on a felony crime. You can still be prosecuted for the murder of Tito. You are running from this town as much as you are going to college. We both know what you did here that is making you run. When I find evidence of what you did, you will have to stop, and that is when I will bring you down. I'm a patient man, and sooner or later, my patience will pay off."

It appears it was O'Neil who was given a warning at the *Blanket Party,* and from his angry response, it is clear that he got more than a warning. They probably beat the living daylights out of him. Tim now realizes he shouldn't have provoked the angry tiger.

"Pardon me, if I don't wish you success," Tim responds as he continues walking and returns home to begin packing his suitcase in preparation for tomorrow's ride to Farmingdale State College.

Chapter 44

On a Yellow September Day

On an unusually warm and sunny day in September just one week after Tim has left Dobbs Ferry to attend college, Jane Ferrari, on her way to the bakery, passes by the aqueduct. When she looks down at the familiar path, an emaciated dog can be seen limping with its head down and walking in her direction. Jane can't believe her eyes. Despite its weathered and beaten look, Jane recognizes Daisy immediately. "Daisy! Daisy!" she yells out. Daisy lifts her head and begins to bark, while she attempts to move at a faster pace.

"Oh Daisy, look at you. Where have you been?" she asks as she kneels, and Daisy jumps into her arms. "Tim has been looking for you for almost a year. He will be so glad to hear you are alive. How in God's name have you survived this long?" The meeting is most timely. Daisy has barely survived the year in the woods, has abandoned her pack of dogs that has dwindled to a mere three, and wants to return home. Jane decides to stop at the hardware store and buy a leash and collar for Daisy before she goes to the bakery.

When Louie Miller sees Jane enter the hardware store with Daisy, he quickly fills a bowl with water. Daisy laps up the entire bowl of water without stopping to breathe.

"Is this possibly the dog Tim had lost last year?" Louie asks.

"Yes, and she has survived living in the woods for almost a year," responds Jane.

"Well, here are some very sharp scissors to cut off some of her matted hair after you bathe her. Now, I hope you take her home and give her all the attention she needs. She surely deserves it."

"I will, Mr. Miller, I will."

While Jane is busy at Miller's hardware store, Johnny Pacetti is making his way up Main Street.

When he stops to rest for a minute, Mrs. Rossi exits the bakery five feet away from him.

"Good morning, Mrs. Rossi. Isn't it a great day?" Johnny exclaims in his typical long drawn-out voice.

Marie Rossi has found little joy in chatting with anyone since her daughter's death, but somehow Johnny's excitement about just being alive has always given her spirits a lift.

"It certainly is a beautiful day, Johnny," she responds.

"Have a nice day, Mrs. Rossi."

"And you too, Johnny."

After buying a leash and collar, Jane fits the collar around Daisy's neck, attaches the leash, and continues down Main Street with Daisy at her side. Halfway down the street, Johnny Pacetti approaches her.

Johnny's eyes light up, and his eyebrows lift as he inhales, and then he begins to speak.

"Jane Ferrari, how is your brother Tim? Tim was born on September 27, 1942 and you were born on May 31, 1941. Where is your brother Tim?" Johnny asks.

"He left the village to go to college," Jane responds. "I'll tell him you were asking for him."

"Hi, Daisy," Johnny says, and Daisy walks over to Johnny so he can pat her on the head.

Taken aback, Jane asks, "How do you know Daisy?"

"She's Tim's dog."

"Did you know she has been missing?"

"She can't be missing. She likes to sit next to me when I'm in the woods, looking for Indian arrowheads. I see her all the time. It's good to see you and Daisy on a yellow day," responds Johnny. "I knew it was going to be a good day today. That is why I wore yellow."

Johnny opens his jacket, and he is wearing a yellow shirt, yellow socks, and a yellow belt identical to Tim's yellow belt, only it is a much larger size, and the last hole in his belt is enlarged. The hole is big enough to run a rope through it and the belt is thick and strong enough to hold up Johnny's pants or to be used as a hangman's noose when attached to a rope.

"Did Tim give you his belt?" Jane asks.

"No, I have my own belt for yellow days," responds Johnny. "I haven't worn it for a long time."

"How did the last hole in your belt get so large?" Jane asks.

"It's a secret. I can't tell you."

"Well, Johnny, I can fix it," she responds, while she reaches out and is able to cut his belt with her new scissors removing the enlarged hole. "Doesn't that look a lot better, Johnny? Now, no one is going to ask you about your secret."

Johnny jumps back, and his eyes open wide again.

"I don't need that last hole to hold up my pants, do I?" he responds.

"No, you don't, Johnny."

"Thank you, Jane. Have a nice yellow day."

The meek and defenseless in this world often suffer at the hands of others. Seldom are they able to protect themselves or to fight back. On rare occasions, after being endlessly subjected to the will of others, they will unexpectedly throw caution to the wind and find that God-given inner strength necessary to take up arms against their adversaries, while the unsuspecting rest of the world remain unaware of their actions.

Aggressive individuals who find great joy in taking advantage of the defenseless should take heed that life on earth is too short to waste precious time creating misery for others. In the end, the ill will they create will give them little comfort, and their actions may lead them in a direction that will cause them to leave this world much sooner than they can imagine.

Chapter 45

The Future

Veronica, unfortunately, will be wrong about her recovery from depression. Over the remaining thirty-six years of her life, she will have to take at least a dozen other drugs for depression. The doctors will prescribe a new drug whenever the one she is taking becomes ineffective. As she gets older, the length of time in between downtimes will get shorter and shorter. She will continue to battle her way out of each down episode until the very end. She will die at the age of eighty-seven.

Within a few years, Boo's drinking will lead to a near-death operation. He will stop drinking and become a grandfather to ten grandchildren, collect coins, and maintain a vegetable garden that will produce prize tomatoes for forty more years. He will die at the age of ninety-three.

Three years after leaving for college, Tim will ask Joan out, and she will accept. He will make a complete ass of himself and will able to move on with his life after his last date with Joan. Tim will never again live in Dobbs Ferry. He will move to New Jersey after giving up on becoming a commercial artist and will receive a degree in mathematics. He will eventually start his own computer consulting company and remain in New Jersey.

Rick Squilera and Tim will become best of friends during their college years. Rick will join IBM after college. He will never have the time to write his book. He will die far too young for such a talented and genuinely good human being.

Johnny Pacetti will live for twenty more years before he quietly passes away. He will never tell anyone his secret except Tim Ferrari the day after Tito's body was found. Tim had him swear he would not tell his secret to anyone else. He never did. Tim never asked him how or why he killed Tito. His huge collection of Indian arrowheads will be donated to the Friend's of Wicker's Creek.

Rosanne Carrero will never tell anyone what happened to her or what she did in return. Despite not being able to see the executioner's face, the yellow belt had convinced her it was Tim she saw from across the aqueduct on that fateful day. She still believes that it was Tim Ferrari who had rid the world of a brutal young man, who didn't deserve to live.

Detective Dan O'Neil, for years, will continue to search for evidence that will implicate Tim Ferrari in the death of Tito Menetti. During that time, he will question Father John on several occasions. Father John will pretend he is half deaf and shell shocked, and he will be unable to answer Detective O'Neil's questions. "God bless him!" Johnny Pacetti will never be interviewed.

Officer Raymond McEntire will win the lottery, move to California, and become a surfer.

Officer Tony Romano will become the chief of police in Dobbs Ferry, and Detective O'Neil will report to him.

Detective Pascutti will be hired by the New York City Police Department and will become famous for solving many of New York City's cold cases.

Father John and Blackie will both die before the age of fifty-five. Like so many of the men of WWII, they not only protected us by going off to war, on returning home, they remained silent to avoid exposing us to the its horrors and to man's inhumanity in times of war.

Mike Campi will leave the New York area in 1976 and move to Georgia, where he will open an Italian restaurant and become famous for his seafood crepes.

Don Sandino will have four years of success in college sports. He will eventually move to Albany, where he will lead a conservative party and become the Mayor of Albany.

Starkey will move to New Jersey after attending college. He will become a partner in an accounting firm. After retiring, he will return to Westchester New York, where he will work part-time for a country club as caddy master and will report to the assistant pro.

Frank Tulio will become a New York fireman. He will eventually retire and move to a town near Lake Erie where he will be recognized for his fishing and hunting expertise.

Freddie Kerry will stay in Dobbs Ferry. He will become a member of the Friends of the Old Croton Aqueduct, a preservation group.

Bill Moretti will attend college in Connecticut, where he will become a warden at a state penitentiary. No one will ever escape the prison, while he is in charge.

Nicky Trapiani will move to the south, own a successful meat market, and one day become the number one amateur bicyclist over the age 65 on the east coast.

Like the Weckquaesgeek, Tim's brothers, sister, and many of their children will move north of Westchester to the land of the Wappinger tribes. Increased property taxes will make it difficult for retires or newlyweds to own a home in Dobbs Ferry.

Daisy will be reunited with Tim. She will live to the age of eighteen and will never leave home again.

In the 1980s, the Dobbs Ferry football team will be voted Westchester County's team of the decade after winning nine sectional titles and having a forty-two game winning streak. It remains the longest high school football-winning streak in state history and is one short of the national high school football record. In the last decade, Dobbs Ferry has won four state championships. Two of the star players are the Irish and Italian grandsons of men that played on the Dobbs Ferry football team in the 1950s.

In 1968, the New York State Office of Parks will purchase 26.2 of the 41 miles of aqueduct from New York City to create the Old Croton Aqueduct State Historic Park that is now a public hiking trail, running from Yonkers to the Croton Dam in Cortlandt, New York.